They must not know who I am . . .

Cleo knew eavesdropping wasn't really polite, but her curiosity got the best of her.

"Looks like it might be a close race between you and Jason," Michael said.

"He doesn't have a chance," said Charles.

"I admit, you'll probably pull it off, but you never know, Jason's got a lot of friends," said Andy.

Charles looked around and lowered his voice, "I don't just *think* I'm gonna win, I *know*. I'm working on a plan and I'm gonna need your help."

Cleo's heart raced. *I shouldn't be hearing this,* she thought. But she wasn't able to leave now.

Andy looked confused. "Um, what are you talking about?"

Cleo leaned over, ever so slightly, not wanting to miss a word.

"I'm telling you," Charles said. "I know how to rig the election. You're looking at your next student body president."

UNDERCOVER CLEO

ANNE SCOTT

BERKLEY BOOKS, NEW YORK

UNDERCOVER CLEO

A Berkley Book / published by arrangement with the authors

PRINTING HISTORY
Berkley edition / September 1995

ISBN: 0-425-14967-6

BERKLEY®
Berkley Books are published by The Berkley Publishing Group, 200 Madison Avenue, New York, New York 10016.
BERKLEY and the "B" design are trademarks belonging to Berkley Publishing Corporation.

PRINTED IN THE UNITED STATES OF AMERICA

10 9 8 7 6 5 4 3 2 1

Many thanks to
Suzie, Ivy, and Laura Anne
for their help and encouragement.

Chapter 1

"Why can't I be like everyone else?" Cleo Oliver moaned as she stood in front of the full-length mirror in her room. Full length for Cleo was a whopping five feet nine inches and at thirteen years old she was, to her great dismay, still growing.

Taking a few steps back, she practiced some of her "look shorter" poses. Cleo had become an expert on those since her growth spurt had started two years ago, but nothing seemed to help today. The spindly bean-stalk that was her reflection still stared back at her from the mirror.

"I must be an alien," she muttered. "I look like something that just stepped out of a UFO." Besides towering over the other girls in her class by a good half a foot, Cleo was also quite a bit thinner. Together with her unruly black hair, huge green eyes that changed color from day to day, and rather sculpted face, she didn't look like anyone else her age.

"Cleo?" Her mother's voice came from down the hall. "Could I see you when you have a minute?"

"Sure, Mom, be right there," called Cleo. "Just let me change my clothes." It was Sunday morning and Cleo was still in her pajamas. She grabbed her favorite jeans off her "cuddy" chair—the place where, when she was little, she used to sit and cuddle with her mom or dad as they read her stories.

The Early American wing-backed chair with maroon flower-patterned cushions and a ruffle around the bottom matched nothing else in the room, but there was no question that it belonged. Cleo preferred antiques to the coordinated bedroom sets of her friends. Everything in her room, from the Chinese wedding bed to the early 1800s sewing table that served as her nightstand, was special in some way. She liked to imagine the history of each of her pieces—to wonder who had sat in her chair, who had slept in her bed, who had read by the light of her lamp.

Cleo plopped herself onto the cuddy chair, prompting an appearance from Phoebe, her pet mini-lop rabbit, who spent part of each morning napping under the skirt of the chair.

"Hey, Phoebe," Cleo crooned as she picked up the animal. "I guess you're a giant just like me, huh?" The tan, floppy-eared beast, who had free run of the apartment and used a litter box just like a cat, had surpassed expectations and grown from a cute little bunny that fit in Cleo's hand into an enormous, though still quite huggable, ten-pound rabbit.

Cleo kissed her pet, then set the animal back on the floor. She pulled on the jeans and an old T-shirt of her father's, then sighed as she noticed her jeans were getting too short. What a way to start off the eighth grade.

The teenager found her mother in the master bedroom at the end of the hall. Mrs. Oliver, or Alexa as she was known professionally, was an internationally famous model, with the long legs and slim figure of a ballet dancer, but her trademark was her hair. There were a hundred different shades of red and brown blended together in Alexa's famous chestnut tresses, and when combined with her bright green eyes and perfect creamy complexion, the result was a startling beauty unlike anyone else's.

Right now Mrs. Oliver was packing the last of three suitcases for her trip to Paris later that day. In addition to a magazine photo shoot, Mrs. Oliver would be taking part in a fashion show where many of the top designers would be showing a special collection as a benefit for a children's hospital.

"You wanted to see me?" asked Cleo.

"Hi, honey," said her mother without looking up. "Listen, my plane doesn't leave until six-thirty so I thought we could do something together this afternoon. Maybe go shopping? Or I could take you to lunch."

"Well," Cleo hesitated, "Robbi's coming over." Robbi Richards was Cleo's best friend and the two girls were inseparable during off-school hours.

"She can come, too. We'll make it 'girls day out' since your father is busy finishing up his report on the campaign,'' said Mrs. Oliver as she adjusted an earring.

''Thanks, Mom, but we sorta have plans. Could we do it when you get back?'' Cleo felt bad about turning down the offer, but the girls had been looking forward to meeting Boy George that afternoon. The singer was going to be at Gutenberg Books on Fifth Avenue signing his autobiography, and with Robbi's latest passion being eighties music, she was dying to meet him.

''Of course, honey.'' Mrs. Oliver stood up and looked at her daughter. ''And, Cleo . . . ?''

''Yes?''

''Don't slouch.''

Cleo rolled her eyes at the familiar phrase. She shuffled to her parents' bed and flopped herself down.

''Cleo, what's the matter?'' Mrs. Oliver inquired as she sat next to her daughter.

''Nothing. It's just that I'm so tall and goony.'' Cleo's eyes filled with tears. ''Mom, am I ever going to stop growing?''

''Oh, Cleo, is that what's bothering you? Of course you'll stop growing someday, but I wouldn't worry about being too tall yet. Girls just mature faster than boys, but I promise you, they'll catch up in a few years.''

''Mom, I don't care about boys. I just want to fit in with my friends. You know what the kids at school call me?''

''What?''

'' 'The Giraffe'!''

Mrs. Oliver chuckled a little sadly. ''Yes, I remember being called something like that myself.'' She was five feet eleven inches, a fact that didn't give Cleo much comfort. "Cleo, look at me."

Cleo sat up and looked at her mother.

"When I was your age, I was a head taller than everyone else in my class, too," continued Mrs. Oliver. "I know what it's like, but believe me, things will get better."

"Mo-o-mmm." Cleo clapped her hand over her eyes in frustration. Her mother was always saying that she understood, but how could she? Alexa was so perfect and beautiful, and besides, everyone adored her. Cleo found it hard to believe her mom had ever been a teenager, let alone one who got teased at school.

"I know, I know. That doesn't help you now. You just want to be like everyone else, right? But, honey, if you're already different, why not make the most of it? Here, let me show you how to use what you have to your advantage." Mrs. Oliver took Cleo's hand and led her to the vanity table.

Cleo's mother started to get so excited that Cleo couldn't help cracking a smile as well. "Believe it or not, I hate wearing makeup, but unfortunately, it's part of my job description. The real trick is to make it look like you're not wearing any. Now, close your eyes."

Mrs. Oliver carefully applied eye shadow and liner. "Okay, open them and look down . . . look up," she said as mascara went on. Subtle blush, lip liner, and lipstick completed the job.

"What do you think?" Cleo's mom asked.

Cleo gasped. It had been just fifteen minutes, but now she looked like one of the women in the magazines—like her mother. "Wow!"

"Do you see what we did?" Mrs. Oliver asked. "With a little contouring to highlight your cheekbones, and darker shades of eye shadow and lipstick, we've brought out your best features, and added a few years to your face.

"Now . . . your hair. I think just a simple twist." And in two minutes, Cleo was looking at a remarkably older and more sophisticated reflection of herself in her mother's vanity mirror.

"I look so . . . pretty," Cleo said.

"You *are* pretty, Cleo, with or without makeup. But I wanted to give you a glimpse of how you might look in the not-so-distant future, and maybe get you thinking about all your possibilities."

"Mom, this is definitely better than I looked a few minutes ago."

Mrs. Oliver placed her hand on her daughter's shoulder. "That's because you're not seeing the whole picture, Cleo. You have genuine beauty, the kind that can only come from the inside and that will always shine through, no matter what you look like outside. Cultivate that and you'll be comfortable with yourself. That's really the best way to fit in at school, or anywhere for that matter. Remember, all the makeup in the world can't cover a nasty personality."

Cleo gave her mother a disbelieving look.

"I know, I *do* earn a living as a model," said her mom, "but I'm not going to be able to do that forever and the people who really love me, like you and Dad, aren't the ones who pay me to show off their clothes."

While Cleo was staring at her now rather glamorous face, the doorbell rang. "It must be Robbi," said Cleo. "I'll be right back, Mom," and she ran to answer the door.

As she got to the foyer, she had an idea. Pulling one of her mother's coats off a hanger in the coat closet, Cleo wrapped it around herself and dramatically swung open the door.

Robbi stood there, eyes closed, singing much too loudly to the music on her Walkman. Decked out in an old tuxedo shirt of her brother's, cutoffs with a wide seventies tie as a belt, striped knee socks, and green sneakers, Cleo's best friend was one of those kids who was completely self-assured even at age thirteen. Robbi never worried or cared about fitting in, but did everything with such confidence that she always seemed to be on the cutting edge. Being half Japanese, she had a wonderfully exotic face, and Cleo thought that at four feet ten inches, Robbi was the perfect size.

"Hi, Mrs. Oliv . . ." Robbi stopped and looked again. "Cleo? Cleo! What did you do? You look totally great!"

Cleo laughed. "Did you really think I was my mother?"

"No! Well, maybe at first, but um, I'd know those shoes anywhere."

Cleo glanced at her feet and saw that her red high-top Keds didn't exactly match her mother's chic coat.

"But you look amazing," Robbi continued, "like you're about twenty years old."

"I know. I feel completely weird. Not like myself at all."

"Well, it's fabulous," declared Robbi. "Everything except the shoes."

The girls laughed and walked back to see Mrs. Oliver. Cleo's mother agreed with Robbi that the Keds didn't quite complete the makeover so she put together a stylish outfit using some of Cleo's dressier clothes and pieces from her own wardrobe, including a blouse Cleo especially liked with large hand-carved wooden buttons. As a final touch, Mrs. Oliver brought out a pair of low-heeled suede pumps for Cleo to wear.

Robbi let out a loud wolf whistle. "Boy, wouldn't you like Jason to see you like this!"

"Shut up, Robbi!" Cleo whispered quickly. She'd told Robbi about her crush on Jason Garrett, a boy at school, but she certainly didn't want her mother to know.

Mrs. Oliver tactfully ignored the remarks. "Not bad," she declared as she stood back to admire her daughter. "I don't suppose this is what the average thirteen-year-old is wearing to school, but you know what, Miss Cleopatra Elyse Oliver—you're a knock-out!"

"Oh, Mom, you're just saying that." Cleo looked at herself in the mirror once more. "But I've got to admit, I do look great!"

She and Robbi giggled, then listened as Mrs. Oliver turned serious for a minute. "Now don't start thinking that makeup and fancy clothes are going to solve your troubles, though I'll admit it might boost your mood.

You just remember, if you work at it, there's usually a way to turn what you think are problems into assets."

Cleo hugged her mother. "Thanks, Mom."

"Anytime. But, Cleo . . ."

"Don't slouch!" Cleo chimed in. The trio broke into laughter (though Robbi wasn't quite sure what she was laughing at) and the two girls left to discuss their plans for the afternoon.

Cleo and Robbi had become friends three years ago when the Richards family had moved to New York City from Los Angeles. Both Cleo and Robbi were students at The Walton School, a private, coed institution on the Upper West Side of Manhattan that went from first grade through twelfth. As eighth-graders, Cleo and Robbi were now the upperclassmen of Walton's middle school.

"You should definitely go out like that," proclaimed Robbi.

"Right," Cleo snorted. "And what if someone from school sees me?"

"What about it? You look really beautiful." Robbi had always thought her friend was stunning even if Cleo herself didn't. "Think of it as an adventure!" she continued.

It only took a little prodding before Cleo found herself eager to play "adult." She grabbed her wallet from her backpack and dropped it into a rarely used purse that she swung over her shoulder.

"Bye, Mom! Robbi and I will be back later this afternoon," called Cleo.

"I'm leaving here about five o'clock," said Cleo's

mom, "so if I don't see you, be good while I'm gone. I'll see you Friday morning." Since her mother would be away for two weeks, Cleo would be joining her for a long weekend in Paris.

Mrs. Oliver came out to give her daughter a kiss good-bye. "You look all grown-up."

Cleo smiled at the compliment and stood up a little straighter.

"Well, you two have a good time," said her mother. "And take care of Dad for me, okay?"

"I always do," Cleo said, laughing, as she and Robbi stepped into the elevator.

Cleo and Robbi nodded to the doorman as they stepped into the lobby of the apartment building on Central Park West where the Olivers lived. It was a pre-war co-op with only three large apartments on each floor.

Max, the day doorman, tipped his hat. "Good day, Miss Robbi." Then said, "Ma'am," as he gave Cleo a curious look.

Cleo started to giggle, but Robbi quickly poked her in the ribs. As soon as they got outside, both of them burst into hysterical laughter. "You see, Max didn't even recognize you!" Robbi exclaimed gleefully.

"And he's known me since I was a baby," said Cleo. "If I can fool him, I can fool anyone."

"What do you mean?" asked Robbi.

"Oh, I don't know," answered Cleo with a shrug. "Come on, let's get going."

Chapter 2

Cleo and Robbi walked up 69th Street to Columbus Avenue. Full of trendy clothing stores and fine restaurants, Columbus Avenue had an ever-changing face. Stores appeared and disappeared regularly, but the merchandise was always stylish and usually pricey. There was something for everybody, even if it was just window shopping.

Cars and trucks were double- and triple-parked on both sides of the wide one-way street, while cabs and limousines honked and jockeyed for the best lane. The avenue definitely embodied the spirit of the Upper West Side. This section of New York City was an eclectic assortment of shops and homes, with a little of everything that could be found in Manhattan. There were newer apartment buildings, turn-of-the-century brownstone town houses, and grand, even famous older apartment buildings like the Dakota or the Ansonia Hotel. Twenty years ago the Upper West Side had been a rough neighborhood on the edge of poverty, but the beauty of the area had prevailed and now it was considered one of the most fashionable parts of the city.

The two girls made quite a pair, one tall and elegantly dressed, the other a tiny colorful whirlwind of funky clothing. They made an obligatory detour into the pet store on 72nd Street to visit Sidney, the Scottish Fold cat who was mascot of the place. Sidney was blind, but knew the girls by scent and started purring the moment they walked in. Cleo and Robbi loved the big black and white cat and rarely passed the store without stopping in to scratch his strange flat ears.

Today there was a young couple looking at puppies in the pet store. Both wore black leather jackets and tight black pants and had adorned themselves with metal-studded jewelry and tattoos. Cleo couldn't help staring, amused by the fact that for all their arrogant posturing, the pair spoke in a sort of a baby talk to the puppy, the same as anyone else.

People-watching was a game Cleo had learned from her father and the two often played it while having dinner in one of the many sidewalk cafés along Columbus Avenue. Cleo loved observing different clothing styles, as well as distinctive body postures and facial expressions, and she had fun imagining what mysterious stories might be behind the people she saw. For serious people-watchers, New York was definitely the place to be.

When the couple in leather turned toward the girls, Cleo quickly averted her eyes and concentrated on Sidney. After a hearty dose of cat nuzzling, the girls continued on to the music store.

The Hits, a new music chain store, was three massive floors of cassettes and CDs. One of the neat attractions of the place was the listening stations all around the store that played the newest CDs. The selections were updated regularly and it was fun to sample cuts before deciding what to spend money on.

The girls went directly to the top-sellers rack. If they hadn't dropped by the store in a while, they would start at number fifty and work their way to number one, but since they had been there recently they only checked out the top ten.

"I'm going downstairs to poke around the 'oldies' section," Robbi announced. "Wanna come?"

"Nah, I'll stay up here," said Cleo. "I want to see if there's anything new from MissDirected." She loved the dance music of the four-girl group from Chicago.

When she found their new CD (up to number twenty-three already!), Cleo looked around hopefully for a listening station that was set up with the disc. Near the back of the store she lucked out and found the MissDirected CD at one of a quartet of stations.

She put the headphones on, then pushed the button marked PLAY. It wasn't long before she was nodding her head in rhythm, lost in the close harmonies of the four singers. Turning up the volume a little, she failed to notice the trio of boys heading her way.

Charles Maxwell, Andy Monahan, and Michael Payton were three of the most popular students at Walton. They were the kind of boys to whom everything seemed to come easily. Though Charles was somewhat bossy, people still found themselves attracted to the tall, good-looking boy who was full of charm that he could turn on and off as needed.

Andy was a gifted athlete who played on many of the school teams and Michael was an electronics whiz kid. He was always bragging about some new computer system he had tapped into, and there didn't seem to be a computer or video game he couldn't master in just a few hours. To Cleo all three were completely intimidating.

Charles, Andy, and Michael stopped at the stand right next to Cleo, but she was so engrossed in the third cut of the CD that until Michael stepped back and bumped into her, she had no idea anyone was near.

"Oh, sorry," Michael apologized as he steadied himself.

Cleo replied, "It's all right," and found herself staring at the three boys from her school. Turning away immediately, she ripped the headset off, ready to run in embarrassment. Wearing makeup and her mother's clothes out among strangers on the street was one thing, but she really hadn't expected to see anyone she knew.

The earphone wires caught the wood buttons of her mother's blouse and as Cleo awkwardly tried to untangle herself, she realized, to her surprise, she wasn't hearing any snickering or teasing from Charles and his friends. In fact, she was hearing nothing but the boys' casual conversation. Venturing a peek, Cleo saw that they weren't paying her any attention whatsoever.

They must not know who I am, Cleo thought as she took a deep breath, trying to calm her pounding heart. She was about to walk away nonchalantly when Robbi came bouncing around a corner, saw the boys, and stopped.

To Cleo's horror, a mischievous grin appeared on her friend's face as she headed straight for the group.

"Hi, guys, seen Cleo?" Robbi called out with a gleam in her eyes.

Cleo cringed and made a face at her friend.

"You mean the Jolly Green Giant?" Charles quipped. "Haven't seen her."

Cleo's face fell as the other two boys laughed in appreciation.

Robbi pressed on, "Are you sure?"

"She'd be pretty hard to miss," continued Charles, "but maybe you can't see that high."

The boys and Robbi laughed together, Robbi hardest of all, because she was delighted that Cleo's disguise was working so well.

"You're just a laugh a minute, Charles. Anyway, if you see her, tell her I'll be upstairs." The diminutive girl turned and went toward the escalator, still chortling to herself.

Flustered by Robbi's audaciousness and stinging from Charles's comments, Cleo took a moment to compose herself, intending to join her friend on the second floor. She smoothed her blouse, shifted her purse higher on her shoulder, and was just about to sneak off when she heard Jason's name mentioned in the boys' conversation.

Cleo knew eavesdropping wasn't really polite, but her curiosity got the best of her. Since their talk had to do with Jason—who was, well, sort of important to her—she thought it wouldn't be wrong to listen for just a minute.

"Looks like it might be kind of a close race between you and Garrett," Michael said. Charles and Jason Garrett were running against each other in the upcoming election for student body president.

"He doesn't have a chance," said Charles.

"I admit, you'll probably pull it off, but you never know, Jason's got a lot of friends," said Andy.

Charles looked around and lowered his voice. "I don't just *think* I'm gonna win, I *know*. I'm working on a plan and I'm gonna need your help. Can I count on you guys?"

Cleo's heart raced. *I shouldn't be hearing this,* she thought. But she wasn't about to leave now.

Andy and Michael looked at each other, then back to Charles. "Sure, sure, we're with you."

"Good," said Charles. "It shouldn't tax your abilities too much, but if you guys are up for it, you're going to have to be able to get away next Tuesday night."

Cleo's jaw dropped as she realized what Charles meant. Although the middle school students would be voting Tuesday, ballots wouldn't be counted until Wednesday morning.

Andy looked confused. "Um, what are you talking about?" Andy was a great soccer player, but sometimes he didn't catch on that quickly.

Cleo leaned over, ever so slightly, not wanting to miss a word.

"I'm telling you," Charles said. "I know how to rig the election. You're looking at your next student body president."

Chapter 3

Cleo couldn't believe it. *This has got to be a mistake,* she thought. *Any minute now he'll say it's a joke.* Nothing like this ever happened at Walton.

"You've got to be kidding, Maxwell," said Michael. "Why would you do something that stupid?" Annoyed, he shook his head and put on the earphones at the station.

Charles stared at his two friends. "You know how my dad is. He treats me like a total loser. If I can win . . ." The teenager swallowed hard. "Well, I've got to win and I can't take any chances."

"I don't know." Andy was doubtful.

"What's the problem? I thought you were my friends," demanded Charles.

"Well, yeah, but aren't you asking us to, like, cheat?" said Andy, not sure he liked this at all.

"Not at all, ditzhead. We all know I'll win anyway, this is just insurance." Then Charles gave one of his famous sad smiles. "Look, guys, just forget it. I thought I could depend on you, but I guess I was wrong." He sighed, then turned to leave.

"Wait a minute, hold up, Maxwell. Just let us think about it," Michael yelled, the headphones blasting in his ears.

Charles reached over and turned down the volume for Michael. "Look, Payton, you've been moaning about wanting to head the graduation committee this year. Help me and I'll make sure you're the guy who plans our graduation trip."

Michael Payton took off the headphones and thought about this.

"What would we have to do?" asked Andy Monahan.

"I've got some more details to work out, but I'll let you in on everything tomorrow, okay?" said Charles. "I take it we're still on for The Pizza Palace?"

"Yeah, about five, after Monahan's soccer practice," answered Michael. "Come on. I think I'm gonna buy this CD."

The boys moved away, leaving Cleo standing there completely stunned. Once she was sure they were out of sight, she found Robbi, and the two girls hurried off to meet Boy George. Then later, on the subway platform, as they waited for the train, Cleo filled her friend in on everything she'd overheard.

Robbi's eyes got bigger as she listened to Cleo's account of the boys' conversation. "How do you think they're planning to do it?'' Robbi asked.

"Haven't the faintest, but I'm dying to know,'' said Cleo. "I'd give anything to be at The Pizza Palace tomorrow.''

At home later that afternoon Cleo scrubbed the makeup off her face and brushed out her hair, transforming herself back into the ungainly thirteen-year-old. "Guess it's just you and me again,'' she said to her reflection. *Actually,* she thought, *it's kind of a relief to see the old Cleo.*

She was sprawled on the sofa watching television when her father came through the front door of their apartment.

Scott Oliver was a lanky six feet three inches with an ever-present smile and friendly brown eyes that sparkled through his aviator-style glasses. But in comparison to his wife's famous hair, Mr. Oliver's mop was wavy and black and completely unresponsive to a comb. Cleo often lamented the fact that she had inherited this regrettable feature from her father.

It wasn't just his hair that was rumpled either. Cleo's dad was the disheveled opposite of the impeccable Alexa. Cleo thought her father always looked like he'd just been mugged—tie askew (if there was one), ink stains in the shirt pockets, and papers flying out of his briefcase. It amazed Cleo that none of those documents ever disappeared, but it was rare that her father ever lost anything.

Cleo had to admit though, his appearance seemed especially appropriate for his work. Mr. Oliver was an independent journalist who wrote for *The New York Times* as well as other New York City newspapers, and he usually put in long hours on the job. Cleo's dad had, on many occasions, worked through the night, following up a lead or pounding out a story on his computer to meet a deadline.

"I'm home," he called. "Anybody here?"

"Just me, Dad." Cleo had melted into the couch and was comfortably immobile. "Mom's already gone."

"I guess it's just us for dinner, then," Mr. Oliver said. "Shall I whip up something?"

"Uh, you must be tired," Cleo answered quickly. "Maybe we should order in." She loved her dad but he was not exactly the best cook in the world. In the past he had concocted "gourmet" meals of raisin omelets or tuna fish in spaghetti sauce.

One terrific bonus that came with living in New York City was the incredible variety of take-out food—Indian, Kosher, Thai—you name it, you could get it delivered. Cleo knew that tonight would be the perfect night to pick up the phone.

Over white cardboard cartons of Chinese, Cleo and her father each talked about their day, although Cleo purposely left out the bit about the boys' election plans. She still wasn't sure how serious Charles was, or if she should talk to anyone about it (besides Robbi, of course).

Mr. Oliver's dinner conversation was sometimes complicated and a little boring to Cleo, but tonight her ears pricked up.

"The upcoming mayoral race is turning out to be a real doozy," he said, spearing a large prawn swimming in garlic sauce. "It would take a miracle for the candidates to be able to keep all the campaign promises they've made to their constituents.''

Cleo looked up from her plate piled high with her favorite—noodles in sesame sauce.

''What do you mean, 'promises'?'' she asked, ignoring Phoebe who was up on her hind legs desperately begging for a noodle.

''Oh, you know, honey, some people will say anything to get elected.''

Cleo watched as her dad spilled a bit of black bean sauce down his shirt. It was a regular occurrence. Suppressing a giggle, she probed further.

''Dad, do people ever fix elections?''

''Well, it sometimes happens,'' he replied, ''even though voting procedures are carefully regulated nowadays. However, it used to be fairly common for politicians to try to tamper with the vote.''

''But how would they do it?'' she asked as she gently pushed Phoebe away. The rabbit was now fiercely nudging Cleo's ankle in her quest for food.

''Different ways,'' her father answered. ''Pay people to vote for them, stuff the ballot boxes, or there's a practice called 'repeating' where the same people register to vote in several different counties. Actually, come to think of it, there was a scandal recently involving a city councilman who used an ingenious method to win.

''You see, when people die, their names aren't immediately taken off the list of registered voters. This particular councilman had friends vote for him using the names and ballots of deceased people from his district.'' Cleo's dad clucked. ''It's amazing. Some people will always find a way to cheat.''

Mr. Oliver could talk forever on just about anything and he went off on a tangent elaborating on voting procedures in the nineteenth century. Cleo listened for a minute or two, then tuned out. *He actually thinks this is interesting,* she thought in amazement, before her attention turned to her persistent rabbit.

Phoebe's nose was pointed straight up as she stood high on her hind legs, dancing as clumsily as a trained circus bear. Cleo laughed and finally gave in to her begging pet. She dangled a long sesame noodle from one end and the happy rabbit nibbled away at the other. It disappeared so rapidly that the animal might as well have been slurping the long strand.

After Cleo and her father had eaten their fill, they contemplated their fortune cookies. ''Which one do you want?'' asked Cleo's dad.

Cleo chose one, cracked it open, and pulled out the slim white note. She read it aloud. '' 'Imagination and hard work will get results.' Hmm.'' She folded the small slip of paper in half and tucked it into her jeans pocket.

''Look at mine,'' said Mr. Oliver. ''It says, 'Your daughter will do the dishes.' ''

Cleo laughed as she stood to help her father clean up. After finishing in the kitchen, they went to the TV room. One of Mr. Oliver's favorite movies, *The Return of the Pink Panther*, was being shown on cable and they had a ''date'' to watch it together. Ten minutes into the film, however, Cleo's thoughts drifted back to the events of the afternoon.

I've got to go see Mrs. McMillan and tell her about

this, she thought. Cleo felt sure that the headmistress of the middle school would know what to do and would do what was fair.

On the other hand, thought Cleo, *maybe Charles didn't really mean what he said. Maybe it was just election week jitters. I really shouldn't accuse him of something that serious without being certain. Then again, if he is going to cheat in the election, it wouldn't be right* not *to say something.* Cleo sighed. How could she know for sure?

It was possible Charles would win anyway, but she hoped not. Her vote was going to Jason.

Jason Garrett had recently transferred to Walton from a school in England. His mother taught archaeology at Oxford University and had been invited to Columbia University as a visiting professor this year, so the entire Garrett family had moved to New York. Cleo didn't know Jason very well, but she found she couldn't stop thinking about him.

The problem was that Jason Garrett didn't know Cleo Oliver existed. He sort of nodded to her in the halls, but he never actually said anything to her. Plus, of course, he *was* a few inches shorter than she was.

If only I could be at The Pizza Palace tomorrow, the girl thought to herself, *I could find out if Charles is really planning to go ahead with his scheme.* But she knew the boys wouldn't divulge their game plan if they noticed her anywhere around.

Cleo almost laughed out loud remembering the scene in The Hits earlier that day. *Those guys never recognized me, even though they were staring straight at my face. I was inches away and they never knew.*

It had been so much fun, almost like being invisible. Camouflaged in her mother's clothes and makeup, Cleo felt like she could have done anything that afternoon. Nothing would have been too scary.

That's it! Cleo sat straight up. *I can be there tomorrow when the guys meet. If I can come up with a way to disguise myself, there's no reason I can't be right next to them while they're talking.*

Cleo remembered how her mother had changed her appearance. *Maybe if I use another color lipstick and some of that contouring stuff, I can make myself look different,* she thought. *I'll make myself up to look like one of the regular Pizza Palace customers.*

After school, The Pizza Palace was usually filled with Walton students, but Cleo was afraid that because of her height, she would be recognized if she dressed up as another kid. *What other kinds of people show up in the place?* Cleo asked herself.

An ear-to-ear grin spread over her face as she came up with a solution. *Perfect*, she thought. *Now if only I'm up to playing the part.*

Happy that she might be able to help Jason, Cleo turned her attention back to the movie.

"Great scene coming up, Cleo." Mr. Oliver had fallen into his slightly annoying habit of commenting during movies. He guffawed at Inspector Clouseau's inept antics as the man operated undercover, disguised as a telephone repairman. Cleo watched and made a silent wish, *Please don't let me look that silly tomorrow.*

Chapter 4

Worrying about her scheme to spy on Charles and his friends kept Cleo awake most of the night, so that when her alarm rang the next morning, she was already up and dressed for school. After quickly gathering her books, she went out to the kitchen and found Nortrud was already there, whipping up a batch of banana pancakes for Cleo and her father.

Nortrud, the Olivers' housekeeper, had been with the family since Cleo was born. She was a large-boned woman in her mid-fifties with wild, wiry hair that was dyed in varying shades of red—that is, whenever she remembered. Nortrud's occasional absentmindedness was her only failing, but other than that she was an excellent cook and housekeeper who took her responsibility to the Olivers quite seriously. As far as Nortrud was concerned, the family couldn't live without her.

The housekeeper constantly fussed at Mr. Oliver for leaving a mess wherever he went, at Mrs. Oliver for not eating enough, and at Cleo for everything from homework to table manners, but she loved them all dearly, and if it was possible, they loved Nortrud more. Whenever Cleo's mother was away, Nortrud came a little earlier and stayed a little later to make sure the Oliver household ran smoothly.

"You're up early this morning, missy. Here, have some pancakes and juice," said Nortrud as Cleo took one pancake. "Take more than that or you'll be as skinny as your mother." The woman piled two more pancakes on Cleo's plate.

Cleo's dad was already at the table, trying to rub a syrup drip off of his tie. "Good morning, sweetheart," he said cheerfully. He put his napkin back in his lap, then stuffed a huge bite of pancake into his mouth. "Mmmmm! Nortrud, these are scrumptious."

"Don't eat too fast," scolded the housekeeper. Nortrud often warned Mr. Oliver about his bad habit of bolting his food.

Cleo ate her breakfast, then grabbed her lunch bag off the counter. "I'd better get going. I promised Robbi I'd meet her early." Cleo wanted to find out what her friend thought about her plan to dress up and be at The Pizza Palace this afternoon.

"Okay," said her father. "See you later."

Cleo kissed her dad, gave Nortrud a big hug, and dashed for the elevator.

• • •

The Walton School was an old brick building that took up more than half a city block on the Upper West Side. Part of the structure dated from the 1700s, although the school had begun even further back in 1658 when New York City was only a tiny Dutch settlement called New Amsterdam, and students met in the community block-house.

In the original building was a chapel where graduation ceremonies took place and church services were held on Sundays. Though the school building had been renovated a number of times, it still retained the flavor of a grand old home—small rooms and winding staircases loaded with history, tradition, and ghosts.

Cleo found Robbi in the fourth-floor hallway and let her friend in on her plan.

"So, what do you think?" Cleo asked.

"You're really going to spy on the Three Stooges?"

"I have to. It's just too important."

"I love it!" exclaimed Robbi.

"Do you think you could help me get ready?" asked Cleo.

"Are you kidding? I can't wait," her friend cried. "Maybe we should get started now. I wouldn't mind missing history today."

Cleo laughed and agreed it was going to be torturous getting through the day of classes. The two girls planned to meet after school at Robbi's house where they would have the place to themselves. Cleo didn't think it would be a good idea to experiment with clothes and makeup under Nortrud's watchful eye.

Once school was out for the day, Cleo hurried home as fast as she could. Rooting around in her bedroom closet, she came up with several pairs of shoes, pants, skirts, blouses, and a black baseball cap. Attacking her dresser drawers she grabbed smaller items of clothing and some hair accessories.

A moment later the jewelry box on top of her dresser caught her eye. Opening the lid, she scrutinized several bangle bracelets and after a moment's thought picked up her good luck charm, a necklace with an oval-shaped silver locket that was a gift from her favorite uncle.

Uncle Lionel was Cleo's mom's older brother. He loved to bicycle through foreign countries and the beautiful filigree locket was from his recent trip to Russia. Supposedly it had once belonged to a young tsarina. Cleo clasped the locket around her neck, thinking, *A little good luck won't hurt today.*

Everything else disappeared into her black overnight bag. Cleo looked at the contents and crinkled her forehead as she thought, *It's not enough.*

Mr. and Mrs. Oliver's walk-in closet had once been the smaller half of a bedroom suite. The apartment had been built during the Victorian era, when men and women had separate bedrooms joined by a common bathroom, but the Olivers had converted the smaller bedroom into a large closet. Cleo looked over the shelves and racks of her mother's clothes and she grabbed a long silk scarf and a pair of dark sunglasses that her mother had often loaned her. Perfect! After scanning the vanity, she borrowed a bright red lipstick.

Cleo's bag was stuffed so full she could hardly pick it up. Glancing at the clock on her mother's bedside table, she saw that time was running short, so she zipped the bag shut, hoisted it over her shoulder, and rushed out the front door. On the way to the Richardses' brownstone Cleo made a quick stop at the newsstand on the corner for one very important part of her disguise.

By the time Cleo got to Robbi's house, her friend was so excited she was hopping around like a Mexican jumping bean. Cleo knew that the more outrageous something was, the more her friend got into it, and planning to spy on Charles Maxwell had Robbi ready for takeoff.

Cleo opened her bag and ceremoniously dumped the contents on her friend's bed. Robbi studied the collection, then added a generous amount of oddball accessories to the pile, and within minutes, clothes and shoes were flying. After a flurry of mix and match, plus a half hour of experimenting with Mrs. Oliver's makeup pointers, the girls were finished.

"Ta da," Robbi sang.

Cleo stepped back and checked out her reflection in the mirror. She had pulled her hair back in a high ponytail, then put on red lipstick and plenty of black mascara. Sunglasses rested on the top of her head, but most importantly, Cleo had donned a denim show jacket that Robbi had borrowed from her mother, who was an actor.

These baseball-style jackets had the logo of a play

or musical embroidered on the back and the performer's name on the front. Wearing a show jacket, which was usually black wool with leather sleeves and collars, was a great way for an actor to show the world that he or she was working in a theater production. Cleo rolled the sleeves up to her elbows, threw her black bag over her shoulder, and instantly became indistinguishable from the scores of Broadway hopefuls who lived on the Upper West Side or came into the area for dance classes.

"What do you think?" Cleo hoped she appeared more convincing than she felt.

"This is too cool," said Robbi. "I mean, you're actually going undercover and all, like in the movies. 'Cleo Oliver, Undercover Agent.' No, no, no, I've got it . . . 'Undercover Cleo'!"

Cleo grinned at her friend and repeated thoughtfully, "Undercover Cleo."

Cleo was nervous, but soon found that being in costume gave her a nice feeling of confidence. There was more determination in her walk and she held her chin up, setting her head at a cocky angle. Her mother's scarf, sleekly knotted around her neck, flew behind Cleo as she strode jauntily toward The Pizza Palace.

Walking in the door at a quarter to five, she took a seat by the corner where she knew Charles and his friends usually sat. "I'm doing this for a good cause," she whispered to herself for a dose of extra courage. She ordered a soda and some fries and pulled out the crowning touch to her costume, a copy of *Back Stage*, the entertainment newspaper she had picked up at the newsstand. Cleo had often seen actors in the area poring over the paper and now, like a pro, she popped it open to the audition section and waited for the boys to show up.

About twenty minutes later Charles, Andy, and Michael burst in and seated themselves in their usual corner, barely two feet from Cleo. Her heart beating at a record pace, she held up the newspaper slightly higher and tried to keep her hands from shaking.

Undercover Cleo was ready for action.

Chapter 5

"So, guys, are you ready for my brilliant plan?" asked Charles.

Cleo held her breath. There had been no mistake. Charles meant business and now Cleo wasn't so sure she wanted to hear about it. The knowledge suddenly seemed like a lot of responsibility, but as she looked around, she realized it was too late to leave.

"Yeah, Maxwell," said Michael. "What's the deal?"

A cunning smirk appeared on Charles's face. "I'll need your help to get some keys from Slovenski. Those keys are going to make it all happen." Mr. Slovenski was the nit-picking custodian who had been with Walton forever.

"What?" asked Andy.

"It's actually very simple," said Charles. "Even you

should be able to grasp the situation, Monahan. The keys will get us into Ms. Appleby's office where we will grab a sample ballot, which we will then make copies of, so we can fill them in with votes for me, naturally. After that, we use the keys to get us into school next Tuesday night when all we have to do is get our hands on the ballot box, dump the real ballots, and refill it with our set of votes. Is that beautiful or what?''

"You want us to break into school?" asked Michael.

"If we have a key, it's not exactly breaking in, bozo," Charles rationalized. "Look, we'll tell our parents we're going to an eight o'clock movie which'll give us plenty of time to get in, switch the ballots, and split."

"Okay, but . . ." started Andy.

"Never mind 'but.' Monahan, you're coming with me Friday," Charles commanded. "When Slovenski goes out for lunch, we slip into his workroom and grab his spare keys. I asked old Slove this morning what he'd do if he ever lost that huge key ring he has. Said he keeps dupes in his room, but the geezer also said he's never had to use them. I guarantee you, he won't even know they're missing."

"This does not sound cool," said Andy. Cleo could see the boy sweating even though there was a fan blowing in the restaurant.

"That shows how much you know," said Charles and he turned to Michael. "Payton, your job, should you have the guts to accept it, is to find out exactly where the ballot box will be kept overnight. You're going to be in McMillan's office tomorrow asking how you can get credit for some of those outside computer classes you're taking, right? I think you should just happen to get curious and ask certain questions about the voting procedures, *comprendo*?''

Cleo was amazed that Charles Maxwell had thought out such an elaborate plan. He never worked that hard on any of his English assignments.

''But the first thing we've got to do is to get those keys. My whole plan hinges on those babies and I'm telling you, there's no way I'm going to lose this election.''

Hearing this brought on a coughing attack for Cleo who had just eaten a bit of french fry. All three boys looked over at her.

Mortified, Cleo tried to stifle the cough with a sip of soda but that only made things worse and she sputtered along with the choking.

''You all right, lady?'' asked Charles.

''Oh, thank you, yes,'' answered Cleo in a Southern accent. ''Guess ah just got a little excited seeing this here audition notice for a musical version of *Gone With the Wind*. Ah just cain't imagine a more perfect show for me, can you, darlin'?'' Cleo pulled off a pretty decent Scarlett O'Hara imitation.

''Yeah, right,'' Charles said, turning away. New York City was full of aspiring actors and Charles Maxwell had many more important things to do than discuss a nonexistent career.

Andy, however, kept his eyes on Cleo. ''Hey, don't I know you?'' he asked.

Cleo's heart stopped and she started fumbling in her bag, looking for money to pay her bill so she could flee.

"Yeah," said Michael as he studied Cleo. "Oh, I got it, you're the lady I bumped into yesterday in The Hits."

"Oh." Cleo coughed once more. "Oh, yes, the music store, am ah right?"

"Uh, yeah," Charles agreed.

"Ah thought ah recognized you fellas. Well, bye y'all," said Cleo as she grabbed her bill and headed for the cash register at the front of the restaurant. It was definitely time to make an exit and besides, she had learned all she needed to know.

With her long legs Cleo practically galloped up the streets to Robbi's brownstone apartment. Being recognized, even if it was only as "the lady from The Hits" had been very scary and she was now anxious to get out of her disguise. As Cleo reached the front door, it opened and Robbi pulled her in.

"So how'd it go? Did you find out anything? What'd they say?" Robbi's questions came like bullets.

Cleo was out of breath from running. "Hold on a minute," she panted and flopped down on the floor. Cleo kicked off her shoes and replayed The Pizza Palace meeting for her friend.

"So what if they recognized you from yesterday, they still didn't know it was you," said Robbi. "And they really thought you were an actor! Unbelievable! I wonder if you could fool someone like an adult. I mean, say you actually went to an audition? You could maybe get a great part in some big movie or something. You know, you really seem to be good at this. Maybe you should try to get an agent or something. . . . ''

"Earth to Robbi," said Cleo, interrupting, "I almost got caught! But what's more important is, what are we going to *do*?" Cleo was astounded. Her friend wasn't focusing on the real problem at all. "We can't let the school election be ruined." Cleo paused before suggesting a solution. "I think we have to tell Mrs. Mc-Millan."

"Uh, maybe you should do that alone," said Robbi. "After all, I never did actually hear any of the guys say anything. All I can do is repeat what you told me."

"Are you kidding?" Cleo cried. "You've got to back me up."

"I'll come to the office with you, but don't you think you'd better talk to Mrs. McMillan alone? Seriously, I wasn't even there," said Robbi. "You know, it would be like 'hearsay.' "

"You've been watching those *Perry Mason* reruns again," Cleo accused her friend, though she realized Robbi was absolutely right. Cleo was going to have to face the headmistress all by herself.

That evening Cleo, still very uncertain about what to do with everything she knew, decided to get a little advice from her father. Stuffing a cookie in her mouth, she made her way to his office.

Mr. Oliver was squinting at the computer screen and talking to himself. Cleo smiled. Her dad looked a little deranged, but she knew that was just the way he worked.

Cleo knocked softly on the open door. "Dad?" she asked cautiously.

"Mmm?" Mr. Oliver answered.

"Can I ask you something?" Cleo ventured.

"Sure, honey, let me finish this up. I'll just be a minute." Her father never glanced up from his work and Cleo realized that when he finished, probably in several hours, he would have completely forgotten that she wanted to talk.

Her dad didn't go away as often or for as long as her mom, so Cleo definitely got to see him more, but sometimes, just sometimes, she wished he would see her more. Mr. Oliver was so tied up in his work that even when he was home, he seemed to be somewhere else. Cleo knew she might as well have been a stranger to him when he was deep into a story. She sighed and ambled off toward her bedroom.

As Cleo lay in bed that night, she thought about the election. It really bugged her that Charles was planning to win by cheating. The more she thought about it, the more upset she got and she decided that she had to talk to Mrs. McMillan tomorrow.

There was no way that Cleo Oliver was going to let Charles Maxwell get away with this.

Chapter 6

Tuesday morning Cleo arrived at school and headed straight for Robbi's locker. She waited for her friend to show up, wanting a dose of reassurance before she faced the headmistress.

Before long, Robbi came dancing her way down the hall. "Ready to save Walton from injustice and corruption?" the tiny teenager sang out as she approached.

"Just tell the whole world about it, why don't you," said Cleo, looking around to see if anyone had heard.

"Oh, sorry," said Robbi, suddenly speaking in whispered tones.

"Come on, let's get this over with." Cleo was getting edgier by the second.

The girls walked toward Mrs. McMillan's office in silence.

Inside the frosted glass door, Cleo asked the headmistress's assistant, Ms. Appleby, if she might be able to see Mrs. McMillan for a few minutes.

"Sure, Cleo. Let me see if she's free," answered Ms. Appleby.

The secretary buzzed Mrs. McMillan on the intercom, then told Cleo to go on in. The girl took one last look at her friend, who flashed a thumbs-up sign for Cleo as she stepped into the back office.

Mrs. McMillan was a sturdy, gray-haired lady who wore polyester suits and sensible orthopedic shoes. The heavy black glasses she favored gave her a stern look, but it was a not-so-well-kept secret that the headmistress was a real softie. This morning she was making notes to herself on a small microcassette recorder, but she clicked it off and smiled as she saw Cleo.

"Good morning, Cleo," she said.

"Good morning, Mrs. McMillan," Cleo answered tentatively.

"What can I do for you?" the headmistress asked.

"Well . . ." Cleo started.

"What is it, dear? Are you in some kind of trouble?" Mrs. McMillan looked concerned.

"Well, not exactly," stammered Cleo. "Well, sort of. I mean, it has to do with trouble, but I'm not the one in it."

"Go on, Cleo," said Mrs. McMillan.

Cleo lowered her eyes. "Well, ma'am, I overheard some of the kids talking, and I think they're planning to rig the election next week. They're going to stuff the ballot box with votes they've filled out."

The headmistress cleared her throat and peered over

the top of her glasses at Cleo. She didn't speak for a full minute. "And who were these students, Cleo?" she asked.

Cleo kept staring down at the ground. "I'd rather not say, Mrs. McMillan, because I'm, uh, not one hundred percent sure." Hearing the uncertainty in her own voice, Cleo nervously blurted out, "But you'll know who they are if they ask you where the ballot box will be locked up next Tuesday night."

Mrs. McMillan put on her strict "headmistress" face. "Now, Cleo, how can you expect me to do anything about this if you won't give me any names? I'm sure you believe you heard something important, but let's think about this. Would these students really lay their plans out in front of you? I'm sure it was nothing but a joke," she decided.

"Trust me, it wasn't a joke, Mrs. McMillan. They have everything all worked out. I can't tell you exactly how I know, but I promise you, I heard everything." Cleo started to panic as she realized Mrs. McMillan wasn't going to believe her.

The headmistress leaned back in her chair and looked at Cleo. She knew Cleo Oliver wasn't the sort of student to make up stories, but this was too far-fetched. Besides, Mrs. McMillan prided herself on instilling strong values and morals among the students at Walton and it was difficult for her to imagine that her teachings could be ignored.

"I will not accuse people of wrongdoings without some sort of proof, Cleo," said the headmistress. "But I will tell you something that should put your mind at rest. It is impossible to fool with the ballot box. I've been here at Walton for fifteen, almost sixteen years now, and I know that on occasion, a student *might* be tempted to do such a reprehensible thing. So, as a precaution, after all the votes have been cast, I always put tape across the box and sign my name on that tape.'' The woman stopped and beamed at her own cleverness. ''After that, I lock the box away overnight. There's absolutely no way the vote can be tampered with. Now I think it's best that you forget all about this and run along to class before you're late.''

With that, Cleo was dismissed. Clutching her books dejectedly, she went out to the waiting area where Robbi was sitting—along with Michael Payton, the computer genius in Charles Maxwell's gang of three.

''Mrs. McMillan can see you now, Michael,'' announced Ms. Appleby. The boy picked up his book bag and pushed his way past Cleo.

Cleo stared at Michael as he passed by, then grabbed Robbi's wrist.

''Come on, let's go,'' she told her friend.

Robbi looked puzzled, but let Cleo pull her out to the hallway. ''What?'' Robbi asked as soon as they were safely out of the office.

''Don't you see? Michael Payton's going in there to find out where the ballot box will be kept next week. Maybe now Mrs. McMillan will believe me,'' Cleo said. ''Robbi, she said she would have to have proof. This just might convince her.''

''I wouldn't count on it,'' said Robbi. ''While I was waiting out there for you, Michael asked Ms. Appleby a few questions about the voting. He already knows where the box will be kept.'' Then Robbi winked. "But so do I.''

The two girls sat down to lunch with only one thing on their minds.

"Adults never take us kids seriously,'' declared Robbi as she opened her plastic lunch container. "I just don't see a way to get the evidence we need for Mrs. McMillan, and without proof, we won't be able to build a solid case to convince anyone that we're telling the truth.'' Robbi was in her TV lawyer mode. Besides *Perry Mason* reruns, she was a fanatic about any movie or television series that involved lawyers.

Cleo nodded her head in agreement. "I know.'' She looked at Robbi's lunch, which was a mound of white rice and another portion of something that looked like a bunch of red fingers with suction cups on them. Robbi picked up one of the things with a pair of chopsticks and put it in her mouth. "What in the world is that you're eating?'' Cleo asked.

"Tako. That means octopus in Japanese. It's great if you dip it in a little soy sauce. You want to try some?'' offered Robbi. She held up a piece for Cleo.

"Uh . . .'' Cleo hesitated while she examined the tiny tentacles.

"Go ahead, you'll like it,'' urged Robbi.

Cleo closed her eyes and popped the octopus in her mouth. It was a little chewy, but also sort of sweet. Actually, once she got past the looks it was pretty good.

"Not bad,'' she conceded. *Leave it to Robbi to bring*

something unusual for lunch, Cleo thought, contemplating her own ham sandwich.

"Told you," said Robbi. "Now, what's the plan?"

"There's only one thing to do—we're going to have to stop Charles ourselves," Cleo resolved.

Robbi nodded in agreement and took another bite of her tako. Then suddenly her eyes widened and she started chewing faster, rushing to swallow. "I've got it. We can use my dad's video camera to tape him getting Mr. Slovenski's keys. Mrs. McMillan will have to believe you then."

"Robbi, think about it," said Cleo. "Do you think Charles is going to let us videotape him?" She shook her head at her friend's silliness. "But hey, you've just given me an idea. What if we hide Mr. Slovenski's extra keys before Charles finds them? We could just hold them for safekeeping and then put them back after the election's over. That way, Charles can't pull off his plan. He said the keys were crucial."

Robbi looked at her friend. "You know, I think that could work. We did it. Whoopee!" She jumped up and twirled around on the bench seat, lost her balance, and fell down in a heap at Cleo's feet.

Cleo couldn't help laughing along with her friend, but she knew there were still a lot of details they had to work out. "We haven't done anything yet, Rob. How do we get Mr. Slovenski away from his room?"

"Easy," said Robbi, climbing back on the bench. "We'll say we saw a mouse in the hall and when he comes to check it out, one of us can grab the keys."

The idea sounded like it would work, but just then

Robbi had to leave for a French Club meeting and Cleo was left alone to review the plan. She realized it would be safer if there was a third person to keep watch— just in case Mr. Slovenski decided to return to his room. But Cleo couldn't think of a single one of her other friends she would trust with this secret, or for that matter another friend who would be willing to help out. Not many people were as loyal as Robbi.

Then, Cleo thought of the perfect person. Someone who would have to believe her. Her heart sped up at the very idea of talking to him—Jason Garrett.

Chapter 7

The moment Cleo left the lunchroom she rushed to the fourth floor where the eighth-graders had their lockers. She planted herself in the center of the hall where Jason was ninety-nine percent sure to cross her path. As she watched classmates rushing back and forth and digging out books from their lockers, it occurred to her that she had never once spoken to Jason, and a small anxiety attack shot into her chest.

Maybe this isn't such a good idea, Cleo thought. *What if he doesn't believe me either? I'll probably get nervous and make a total fool of myself. Actually, now that I think about it, I'm sure Robbi and I could handle the whole thing by ourselves.*

Just when Cleo had completely talked herself out of enlisting Jason's help, he came up the stairs and went to his locker. Cleo took two steps to walk away, then lingered a moment as she heard him joking with a boy at a neighboring locker. Something about Jason's British accent made him sound so much more mature and refined than the other boys at Walton.

Looking back, she watched him casually run his fingers through his wavy brown hair, and suddenly Cleo's thinking got all turned around. She knew she just had to talk to Jason.

What exactly is it about him? she wondered. Well, first there were those long dark lashes that surrounded his brown eyes. Then there was that really cool dimple on the left side of his smile. Plus he was a terrific dresser. He never looked sloppy or geeky like many of the other boys. Today he was even wearing a tie. Cleo knew there weren't many girls in the eighth grade, or even the whole middle school for that matter, who didn't daydream about Jason Garrett.

Just then, he raised his head and saw her staring at him. Horrified at being caught, Cleo looked away, but unexpectedly, Jason smiled and waved. Pleased that he was making the first overture, Cleo tried to swallow the grin she could feel spreading over her face. She lifted her hand to wave back, but just before her arm came all the way up, someone brushed past Cleo, throwing her slightly off balance.

"Hi, Jason. Ready for math?" asked Chandra Fisher as she hooked her wrist into the crook of the boy's elbow. Chandra, the prettiest girl in eighth grade, was a petite brunette who was also the head cheerleader.

It was then that Cleo realized she had never had Jason's attention at all and her motion to wave at the boy turned into the flicking of imaginary stray hairs from her eyes. Although Cleo quickly faced the wall to hide her reddening face, she couldn't miss seeing Chandra strolling off to class, arm in arm, with Jason.

Cleo was dead certain that everyone in the hall had witnessed her gigantic blunder, and she was convinced that the heat, visibly rising from her cheeks, was only making her more conspicuous.

How stupid could I be? she berated herself. *Like Jason Garrett would ever notice me.* She left as rapidly as her long stride would carry her and without knowing how she got there, she somehow found herself sitting in her next class.

Rather than face Jason, Cleo would have preferred to go home and crawl under her favorite blanket, a patchwork quilt that her grandmother had embroidered for her, but Cleo knew Jason would want to know about the plot to ruin the election. By the time the final bell of the day rang, her resolve to talk to Jason had returned.

Again she placed herself on the fourth floor by the door to the stairwell to wait, this time slumping a bit against the wall next to the drinking fountain. She figured if she leaned at enough of an angle, it would bring her height down by as much as four inches. Still too tall, but better.

After what seemed like the entire middle school had tromped through the hall, Jason finally appeared—surrounded by a group of kids. Cleo thought she could feel her heart actually skip several beats and she put her hand over it to calm herself. She hadn't counted on having to pull him away from friends and she suddenly found herself wishing Robbi were there for support. *Please, please let him believe me,* she thought.

Regretfully Cleo had to straighten herself up from her perfectly placed slouch before she could go toward Jason and his friends.

"Um, excuse me, Jason, could I talk to you for a second . . . ?" she asked, her tongue moving much too sluggishly through the question.

The group of kids turned and to Cleo's great embarrassment, Jason's gaze went from her neck slowly upward until their eyes met. Drooping just the slightest bit more, Cleo added, "I mean, that is, if you're not busy or anything."

Jason looked around at his friends and shrugged before answering with a somewhat impatient smile, "I have a moment or two. What is it?"

Cleo dropped her head and stared at her feet. "It's sorta private," she muttered, bringing titters from a girl in Jason's group.

Jason kept his eyes on Cleo as he turned his face toward his friends and said, "Go on ahead, the lot of you. I'll be there straightaway." Cleo held her ground, though she desperately wanted to disappear into the crowd as they ping-ponged their way around her on their way out of the hall. When the area cleared, Jason's raised eyebrows let Cleo know that she had his full attention.

She told him Charles's plan and while Jason listened, nodding politely and even asking questions, it was clear he was anxious to leave. More than once, Cleo saw him glance at his watch, then down the hall before his attention returned to her story. By the time she had finished, his chin was tilted at an angle that she could only read as disbelief. Cleo wished her sinking stomach would take her down through the floor and out of school.

"You don't believe me, do you?" she asked.

"Well, you have to admit, it sounds a bit absurd," said Jason. Seeing the hurt on Cleo's face, he changed his tone quickly. "I'm sorry, I didn't mean to sound so harsh. I do appreciate your telling me and I promise I'll think on it, but I'd better catch up to my friends now." Jason shifted his brown leather backpack up on his shoulder ready to leave. As an afterthought, he turned and asked, "Frightfully sorry, but what did you say your name was?"

Crestfallen, she answered, "Cleo Oliver," and wondered if she would ever in her whole life feel worse than she did at that moment.

"Cleo Oliver," Jason repeated thoughtfully. He smiled at her before sprinting down the hallway.

"Strike two," Cleo said to herself, "Mrs. McMillan and now Jason. Maybe I should quit while I'm ahead."

When Cleo got home from school, Phoebe was snoozing in the TV room, her back pressed against the wall and her large white belly exposed. The mini-lop displayed almost none of the wild animal instincts she had been born with and didn't even bother to wake up when Cleo walked in the room. The girl chuckled quietly and picked up a fine-toothed brush before tiptoeing to her pet, who was in the middle of one of her twice yearly shedding seasons. Cleo started lightly grooming the rabbit who lurched awake, then happily stretched out to her full length of twenty-eight inches.

"Listen, Phoebe, *you* believe me, don't you? You think Charles and his friends are going to rig the election, right?" The rabbit yawned as far as her narrow pink mouth would allow.

"Do you think Robbi and I will be able to pull this thing off by ourselves?" Phoebe answered by licking Cleo's leg industriously.

"Thanks, Bun," she said, running the brush over the rabbit one last time. When the phone rang, Cleo was reluctant to interrupt her pet's show of affection so she didn't move.

"Cleo! It's for you," called Nortrud as she came puffing in from the kitchen. Then she lowered her voice and winked conspiratorially, "It's a boy."

Cleo put down the brush and stood up, automatically primping her hair. A boy? *Who could it be?* she wondered, and thought about the possibilities.

Maybe it was Charles or one of his friends to say they were on to her. But probably it was just Brian Nichols who sat next to her in math and had missed class today.

Cleo cleared her throat quietly before picking up the phone. "Hello," she said, anxious to hear who was on the other side.

"Hello, Cleo? Jason here."

"Oh," Cleo managed to get out. She put her hand over her mouth and squeezed her eyes shut. Only when she was sure her voice wouldn't betray her excitement did she speak again. "Hi, Jason, what's up?"

"Listen, I'm still at my yearbook meeting, but could you possibly meet me at The Pizza Palace for a bit of a chat later on? Say in about half an hour?"

This time Cleo couldn't hide the thrill she felt. "Yeah, sure. Does this mean you believe me now?"

"I, ah . . . really can't talk at the moment. But I'll tell you everything later."

Cleo started to speak again, but the click on the other end of the line told her he was gone. She set the phone down carefully, then burst out in a high whoop.

"Cleo? What is it?" called Nortrud. She came running in from the kitchen again. "Are you all right?"

Cleo laughed. "Yeah," she answered. "Everything is very all right."

"Well," harumphed Nortrud. "I'm glad you're happy, missy. But do you think you might keep it a little more civilized?" The housekeeper's scarf had come off during her sprint and her hair had blown upward like the quills of a porcupine.

Cleo smothered a giggle. "Sorry, Nortrud. Um, I'm going to go out for a little while, okay?"

Nortrud smiled and nodded knowingly. "Just be home before dinner." Then, all of a sudden, a dazed look came over the housekeeper's face and she asked herself, "What was I doing just now?"

Cleo gestured to the silver tray and polishing rags in the woman's hands. "Nortrud, you were in the kitchen."

"Oh, yes, yes, so I was." The housekeeper nodded as she bustled away.

Cleo scooted off to her room and whipped open her closet door. She'd worn a comfortable button-down shirt and khaki pants to school that morning, but nothing less than the perfect outfit would do for her meeting with Jason.

She pulled out blouse after blouse, T-shirt after T-shirt from her closet before finally deciding on a short-sleeved emerald-green sweater of baby-soft cashmere. Uncle Lionel had brought it back from a trip to England and Cleo knew the color complemented her eyes.

She quickly pulled the sweater over her head, then checked the mirror. It worked—her eyes were a luminous green. Then she noticed her cheeks were flushed bright pink—too bright—and she ran for the bathroom where she patted cold water on her face, took one look at her hair, and thought, *It's a disaster, what can I do with it!* Rifling through the drawer by the sink, she found a headband that didn't pinch and pushed it on.

There, she thought, *nice but not too much.* Cleo didn't want Jason thinking that she thought this meeting was any big deal. She smiled at her reflection before heading for the front door.

Cleo felt like she was floating over the sidewalks all the way to the twinkling awning of the school hangout. At The Pizza Palace, Christmas lights shone all year long and today Cleo thought they looked exhilarating.

She entered the restaurant and for a moment was worried that her "date" wasn't there. Then Jason waved to her from a table in the back. Remembering what had happened that afternoon, she double-checked behind herself before waving back. But once Cleo saw he was beckoning to her, she wove her way through the tables, dodging the three servers who scurried back and forth balancing pizzas and burgers over their heads.

"Hello, Cleo," said Jason. "Awfully nice of you to meet me here."

"Sure," said Cleo. *That "sure" was way too eager,* she told herself. *Easy, Cleo, easy.* She knew she must be blushing again so she lowered her head slightly, but resisted an impulse to put her glass of ice water up to her cheek. Thankfully the server chose that moment to take their order.

Cleo asked for a root beer float and while Jason placed his order, she surreptitiously checked out the restaurant, half hoping someone from Walton would notice her sitting with the boy. Seeing just a group of sixth-graders that she barely knew, Cleo turned back to concentrate on what Jason had to say.

"I'm afraid I didn't take you too seriously this afternoon," he started, "but I overheard something during my yearbook meeting. Something I thought you'd like to know about."

"Yeah?"

"You know the student body president is the individual who selects the heads of the various dance committees, yes?"

Cleo nodded, thinking that it almost didn't matter what he said. With that accent, anything would sound great.

"Well, I heard someone boasting a bit, saying she

would definitely be the one who would be planning the Christmas Dance and, believe it or not, the Spring Dance as well. Didn't say how she knew, but she seemed quite certain of it. Cleo, I know *I* wouldn't promise jobs to anyone ahead of time unless I was positive I would win.''

''Who said this?'' asked Cleo.

''Liz Cameron,'' said Jason.

Cleo's eyes widened and she allowed her grin to take over her face. Liz was Charles's current girlfriend and apparently the recipient of another campaign promise. Here was a confirmation that something was up with the election.

''That's great,'' exclaimed Cleo. ''I mean . . . I'm glad you believe me now.'' She looked down and casually stirred some of the vanilla ice cream into her root beer. ''My friend Robbi and I came up with this plan. . . .''

''Oh,'' said Jason, ''no need for you to bother. I'm sure I can handle it myself.''

Cleo wanted to scream. Hadn't Jason heard anything she said this afternoon? ''How?'' she asked. ''I already told you Mrs. McMillan didn't believe me. If you want to stop Charles, you've got to help us.''

Jason seemed shocked by the outburst and Cleo backed down immediately. She didn't know why she was getting so upset over this. If Jason wanted to take care of it, she should just let him.

''Look, never mind,'' said Cleo. ''I guess you've got other people, like Chandra, to help you.'' She knew she sounded petty, but she couldn't help it.

The boy looked up. "That wasn't what I meant," he said quietly and Cleo felt her cheeks redden.

"You know, Chandra and her friends were the first people to include me in their activities," continued Jason, "and they're the ones who encouraged me to run for office, even though I'm a new student here. No one else has really even spoken to me much, though I suppose I haven't really taken the time to get to know them yet either, have I?" He smiled and Cleo realized that in some ways, Jason was as shy as she was. "Listen, I'm not promising anything, but I think I'd like to hear that plan of yours."

Cleo took a sip of her root beer float, then decided to forge ahead. She spilled out the plan she and Robbi had devised, anxious once more for the boy's approval.

"Sounds terrific and I think it could work quite nicely," he said, "but would you mind if I made one suggestion?"

Jason explained that he had an old padlock he would be willing to sacrifice for the cause. "I'll put it on my locker, then tell Mr. Slovenski I've forgotten my key. You know how people do that now and again. While he's cutting the lock for me, you and your friend can pinch the key ring."

Cleo laughed. "Yeah, I guess that does sound better than seeing a mouse in the hall." The plan really seemed foolproof now. Cleo and Jason finished their sodas and arranged to meet in the morning by the lockers.

"Okay, we're on, then," said Jason. There was an awkward pause before he continued, "I'd better get on home. I've got to work up my campaign speech for the assembly next week.''

''Oh, I've got to go, too,'' Cleo hurriedly added. The kids each paid their share of the bill and walked out, bumping into Charles Maxwell and Liz Cameron on their way in.

Liz had curly blond hair and bright blue eyes, which she kept wide open, giving her face a perpetually surprised expression, and her fingernails, never bitten down or broken, were painted to match the bubble gum-pink lipstick on her perfect little bow of a mouth. She almost always wore frilly clothing in pastel colors so Robbi had dubbed her ''Baby Doll'' and Cleo had to agree, the term fit to a tee. When Liz saw Cleo and Jason together her eyebrows lifted almost to her hairline.

Liz was spiraled around Charles's arm and he had to shrug her off before speaking to Jason. ''Hey, Garrett, trying to buy the Skyscraper's vote? Here's a hint, free of charge—even with an occasional nerd voting for you, you'll never win.''

Cleo bit her lip to keep from crying.

''I hope you weren't speaking about my friend, Cleo Oliver,'' said Jason, taking a step toward Charles, who for once had nothing to say.

''Oh, come on, Charles,'' said Liz in her high breathy voice, ''let's get a table.'' She gave Jason one of her most flirtatious smiles and pretended not to notice Cleo at all.

''Yeah, you're right, Liz,'' Charles said with a laugh, ''why spend time with losers?'' The two of them turned and pushed their way to Charles's favorite table.

"Beastly chap, isn't he?" said Jason. "Listen, I'm terribly sorry for what he said about you."

"It's nothing, I'm used to it," lied Cleo. "Well, look, I'd better go. See you tomorrow, okay?"

"Yes, see you tomorrow, Cleo Oliver. And thank you." The grin he flashed at her, dimple and all, made Cleo forget that Charles or elections ever existed.

As Cleo entered her apartment she was singing her favorite MissDirected number. Normally she hummed quietly, but today she understood what it meant when people wrote about wanting to break into song.

She stopped by the kitchen, grabbed the portable phone, and, on her way to her bedroom, punched in Robbi's phone number. She couldn't wait to tell her friend all that had happened since lunch. It rang only once before Robbi picked up.

"Hey, Rob," Cleo began, "you'll never guess where I just came from." Without giving her friend a chance to answer, she launched into the events of the afternoon.

"A date with Jason?" cried Robbi. "You've got to tell me everything. Did he, like, hold your hand or kiss you or anything?"

"It wasn't really a *date*," said Cleo. "This was more of a . . . a business thing."

"Right," said Robbi, "and I'm Miss America."

"No, I'm serious, Rob. All we did was talk about the election and how we're gonna stop Charles."

Cleo ignored the "uh-huh"'s spurting from her friend

and filled her in on the new developments. "What we've got to do is get Slovenski's spare keys before the first period bell tomorrow morning. There'll be fewer people around and besides, the sooner we have those keys, the less chance there is of Charles getting them." Then Cleo told Robbi when and where they would meet in the morning.

"Okay, okay, fine, I'll be there."

"Great," said Cleo, and at that moment, she made a decision. There had been one part of the plan she hadn't been able to figure out, but now the answer seemed clear. "Rob, I don't really know how to say this. One of the things we have to do tomorrow is totally important, but a little dangerous. *One* of us is going to have to . . ."

Chapter 8

"Me!" squealed Robbi. "You want *me* to be the one to get the keys out of Mr. Slovenski's room?" There was a clatter in Cleo's ear as the phone on the other end fell to the floor. Cleo held the receiver away from her ear as her friend fumbled for the phone. "Oh, my gosh, this is incredible! I can't believe it."

Cleo had to laugh. "Well, you know how good you are at finding things."

"Oh, yeah. You mean like when I found that TV remote under the radiator at your house? And my father's missing chess piece in his old cowboy boot? Hey, I never thought of it before, but I *am* pretty good finding stuff, aren't I?"

"Yeah, well, I hope your luck holds tomorrow," said Cleo. Robbi did have a knack for finding lost things, but what Cleo didn't say was that her suggestion to have her friend ferret out the keys was also based on the fact that Robbi was so-o-o excitable. Cleo wasn't exactly sure she wanted to be in Slovenski's workroom looking for keys with her high-strung friend as a sentry.

"Oh, my gosh! What am I going to wear? How does a second-story man, woman, I mean, person dress? Cleo, I gotta go. See you."

Cleo clicked off the phone and set it on her desk. She opened her math homework, but found it impossible to concentrate. It seemed like more had happened to her in the past few days than in the whole thirteen years before.

"Oh, no," said Cleo and sat up like a jolt of lightning had hit her. "My journal." She had forgotten all about it in the excitement of the past few days. She closed her textbook—math was definitely a lost cause today—and went over to the bed that was unquestionably her favorite piece in the room.

Cleo had discovered the magnificent piece of furniture herself while on a trip to Singapore with her father, who had been writing a story on the famous Raffles Hotel. The antique Chinese wedding bed was a little on the small side (if one took into account the fact that the bed was originally meant for two people), but it was just the perfect size for Cleo. The piece was hand-carved from the finest teakwood and looked just like a large box, enclosed on the top and three of the sides. Cleo loved to crawl into the one open side of the bed that ran lengthwise with the mattress and faced into the room. Then she could lie on her back and stare up into the teak canopy top that was a maze of intertwining latticework supported by posts carved to resemble bamboo.

Most of all, Cleo adored the headboard. Concealed behind intricate carvings of flowers and animals were all sizes of hidden drawers, perfect for holding a girl's most private secrets. This was where she stashed her leather-bound journal.

She didn't write in it every day, only when she felt the need to confide things too personal for human ears. Cleo was sure that if anyone ever read her journal, they would think she was a real psycho, because most of the time when she wrote, everything around her was either totally great or totally awful. Or she would write on days like today, when something completely out of the ordinary happened.

Cleo turned a little dragon's head that released a narrow, almost invisible drawer close to her pillow from which she slid a dark blue book with a maroon binding. She opened the journal and started to write when she remembered something. Quickly she stood and went to pull her jeans off the hook on the back of her bedroom door. From the pocket she took a white slip of paper— the fortune from her cookie two nights ago.

Carefully she unfolded and reread it, " 'Imagination and hard work will get results.' " It seemed to foretell something important and she decided to tape it into her journal. She wrote for half an hour, then feeling satisfied she had put down all the good parts, she returned the book to its secret compartment and soon after fell into a deep sleep.

• • •

The next morning Cleo was the first to arrive at the meeting place near her locker. As she waited for her friends, she pulled a mirror out of the side pocket of her purple backpack and quickly checked herself in it. She took out lip balm and applied it liberally until her lips shone, then used her fingers to comb through her hair. *Even though Jason and I are only friends, it never hurts to look nice,* she told herself. Just as she was finishing up, the English boy arrived.

"Hello, Cleo." He smiled, taking a slightly rusty padlock out of his backpack to show her. "What do you think?"

"Great," Cleo answered. "You're sure you don't mind?"

"Not in the least. After all, it is for a good cause," he said, looking around. "Where's your friend?"

"Oh, I'm sure she'll be here any minute," said Cleo. Feeling uncomfortable, she shifted her weight to her other foot and anxiously looked down the hall for Robbi. Cleo was torn between wanting her friend to show up to rescue her from having to make conversation with Jason, and wanting to prolong the time alone with him. "What class do you have next?" she asked, immediately thinking, *What a lame question.*

"Science," answered Jason. "Mr. Fleming. I find him exceedingly difficult. Who have you got?"

"For science? Mrs. Garcia. She's pretty good," said Cleo.

"Oh, then you must be in Chandra's class," said

"Now remember, you don't have much time, so hurry!"

As Robbi put her hand on the heavy oak door, her eyes widened until she looked like a baby owl. The hinges were kept well oiled by the custodian and the door swung open silently and easily. The girl stole a last look at her friend, then slipped inside.

Cleo made sure the door was shut, then went down the corridor and pasted her back to a doorway. It seemed like the best place to be inconspicuous and yet be able to see people coming from any direction.

It took Robbi's eyes several seconds to adjust to the dim light in the workshop. There was one dust-filled beam of sunlight coming from a small window high in the wall on the far side of the room.

Her nose wrinkled at the odd smell in the air, a mixture of fuel oil and paint thinners. Hands in front of her to keep from bumping into anything, Robbi shuffled toward a workbench beneath the window. When she reached it, she turned to survey the room. Hanging everywhere from Peg-Boards were screwdrivers, hammers, pliers, bungee cords, rolls of wire, and more. Shelves were crammed with power tools as well as cans of paint and other bottles—the place looked like a well-stocked hardware store. But with growing panic, Robbi noticed there wasn't a key anywhere in sight.

Worried that her time was running out, the girl hopped up onto the worktable, threw open cupboards and felt around on the shelves above. Her fingers darting everywhere, she found lightbulbs, plaster, and electrical cords, but still no sign of anything resembling a key ring.

She was just about to reach on top of the cupboard, when the door to the hall opened and a shaft of light lit up the shelves to her left. Robbi whirled and ducked, ready to leap off the workbench. In her haste, she knocked over a plastic mug with the remains of Mr. Slovenski's morning coffee.

"Find 'em yet?" whispered Cleo through the crack in the door.

"You just gave me a heart attack," said Robbi, then added in a whisper that could be heard two rooms away, "I don't see the keys anywhere!"

Cleo shut the door and started pacing. Checking her watch, she realized three whole minutes had passed. She knew it didn't take very long for Mr. Slovenski to snip a lock and there couldn't be much time left.

Cleo was on the verge of telling Robbi to call it off when Mrs. Garcia, Cleo's science teacher, emerged from a supply room several doors down the hall, her arms loaded with books. The woman staggered toward Cleo.

"Oh, Cleo, thank goodness. Help me carry these upstairs to my room, would you?" said Mrs. Garcia in that particular tone of voice that teachers use to turn a polite request into an order.

Cleo jerked her head in the direction of the woman, then froze.

"Cleo? Did you hear me?" asked Mrs. Garcia.

Cleo's mind shifted into overdrive as she frantically tried to think of some way to warn her friend. *What can I do? What can I do?* Cleo wondered, but absolutely nothing popped into her head as she ran to the teacher's side, just managing to catch several books that were sliding off the top of the pile. Cleo followed Mrs. Garcia up the stairs, throwing a glance over her shoulder and feeling like a total rat as she deserted her best friend.

Robbi, in the cramped work space, was nearing total panic. She had found every kind of tool or device imaginable except keys. Knowing she had only seconds left, Robbi stopped and calmed herself down. She forced herself to think logically, trying to visualize where the custodian might keep a set of keys.

Stepping back, she studied the hopelessly cluttered room. She realized extra keys would be very important, no matter how often Mr. Slovenski did or did not use them, so they would probably be somewhere within easy reach. Her eyes went immediately to a flat wooden cabinet hanging beside the door and half hidden behind an old work apron. Her fingers had just touched the dull brass latch when she heard several male voices outside the door.

"Can you believe it? That bozo Garrett forgot his key. This is too rich. I'm going to have to thank him for helping me win," Charles crowed.

Robbi dropped to the floor, her eyes on an impossible mission to find a hiding place. The broom closet was jammed full and the space under the workbench was filled with boxes—there was nowhere to go. In desperation she tried pulling a large box away from the wall to create a hiding place, but the box was packed with steel pipe and weighed more than she did.

"It stinks in here," said Andy, opening the door and poking his head into the workshop.

"I wouldn't worry about it, Monahan," said Charles, "I'm sure it's environmentally safe and besides, you couldn't have many brain cells left to fry."

The three boys stood just outside the door while Robbi froze, knowing that at any moment, someone might come in and flick on the lights.

A split second before the guys stepped into the room, Robbi dove into a low cupboard that was only half full of old paper bags. The boys hadn't seen her worm her way in but, unfortunately, she hadn't had an extra second to pull the cabinet door shut. Through the opening, she could see Charles enter the room and hit the light switch. Hunched in the shadows, Robbi pulled her toes in toward her body, hoping to make herself microscopic.

She heard Andy complain, "Look, I'm not so sure about this."

"I'm going to pretend I didn't hear that, dork," said Charles. "Just get going and find those keys. We don't exactly have all day. You, too, Payton. I'll stand guard outside and let you know if anyone shows up."

"Maxwell, how come you get the no-risk job?" asked Michael.

"Because I'm the brains of the operation. If Old Bug Face or anybody else comes by, I'm the only one who can sweet-talk them away. Either one of you mush-brains would blow it and we'd all be goners. Now move it."

Andy and Michael ransacked the room, running their hands over shelves and pulling open every drawer in the room, unconcerned about the clatter they were making.

"Nothing!" said Michael. "It must be in one of those cupboards down here."

The small girl's pulse doubled when she heard this and she began breathing so rapidly she was sure the boys were going to hear her. She simply couldn't believe that Cleo hadn't warned her or somehow stopped Charles from coming in.

The open cupboard door right in front of Robbi scared her half to death. She knew she had to do something about the situation, so she gingerly pulled it toward her, a quarter of an inch at a time. The door was almost shut when the hinge creaked.

"What was that?" asked Andy.

Michael raised his head and listened. "I don't know. Maybe a radiator pipe? Come on, come on, Slovenski's going to be back any second."

Michael searched the higher shelves while Andy raced down the line of cabinets coming closer to Robbi's hiding place. Hearing door after door opening and slamming shut, she scrunched farther back into her tiny cubbyhole, certain that at any second, the door was going to fly open and she'd be exposed.

Just then, Andy's voice came from right beside her cupboard. "Last one. They've gotta be in here," he said.

Robbi closed her eyes as the door swung wide open.

Chapter 9

"Got 'em! Let's go, we're outta here," called Michael from across the room. "Right by the light switch, can you believe it?" The triumph was evident in his voice.

Robbi watched Andy pause just on the other side of the wide-open cabinet door. If he dropped his eyes so much as six inches down, she would be caught.

But Andy wasn't thinking of anything except getting out of the musty workroom as fast as possible. He kicked the cabinet door shut and headed off without even a glance in Robbi's direction.

The girl flinched as the door slammed in her face, but she stayed motionless until she was certain the boys were gone. The moment Robbi heard their laughter fade down the hall, she scrambled out of her hiding place and cautiously checked the corridor.

Finding the hallway empty, she headed for the stairs where she collided right into Mrs. McMillan.

"Whoa!" cried the headmistress. "Slow down. How many times do I have to tell you kids not to run in the hallways? You or someone else could get hurt."

"Sorry, Mrs. McMillan," said Robbi as she dusted herself off.

"And what were you doing in the basement anyway?" asked the woman, looking quizzically at Robbi's all-black outfit.

"Well . . ." stammered Robbi.

Just then, Cleo emerged from the stairwell, having overheard the conversation. "Oh, Robbi, thanks for coming down to look for Mr. Slovenski. Jason found him upstairs." She turned to the headmistress. "Morning, Mrs. McMillan."

"Good morning, Cleo," said the woman. "What did you need Mr. Slovenski for?"

"Jason forgot the key for his lock," answered Cleo smoothly, and she smiled while reaching out a hand to grab Robbi. "Come on, we've got to get to math," she said, pulling her friend up the stairs before Mrs. McMillan had a chance to ask any more questions.

"Did you get them?" Cleo whispered as soon as they were out of hearing range of the headmistress.

Robbi glared at Cleo. "Charles and his buds showed up before I could find them," she huffed. "Thanks a lot for watching out for me. Really."

Cleo couldn't have been more shocked. She had been sure that the keys would be kept somewhere in plain sight and it would be a quick in and out job. When

Robbi told her the whole story, Cleo wanted to sit down and cry.

"We're doomed," she said. "Now what do we do?"

Robbi shrugged. "Plan B?"

"Yeah right," said Cleo. "Plan B. Whatever that is."

Cleo and Robbi didn't link up with Jason until after fifth period when they were on their way to lunch.

"So?" he asked.

"Well . . ." said Robbi, "it wasn't really my fault. Circumstances beyond my control, you know?" Cleo rolled her eyes as her friend explained, with far too many embellishments, what had happened in Slovenski's workroom. Robbi had a way of making a story sound exciting, but Jason wasn't buying it.

"Botched it quite nicely, haven't you?" he commented. "So, now what are we to do?"

"Excu-use me, but I didn't see *you* risking your life to find anything in that creepy room," shot Robbi.

"Can we call a time-out?" interrupted Cleo. "Look, we've got two choices here—give up or keep going. I vote that we try something else. What do you two think?"

Robbi brightened immediately. "You mean get the keys back from Charles?"

"No. Obviously we'll need some other plan now, but there's got to be a way to stop these guys if we all work together," said Cleo, putting emphasis on the word "together."

Robbi nodded and Jason with some reluctance also agreed.

"But there's not much time left," Cleo pointed out. "What do you say we meet after school?"

"Well," said Jason, "I've got to be at the soccer game this afternoon, snapping photos for the yearbook. Perhaps we could meet afterward at the playing field."

"Sure," Cleo answered for both girls, "we'll be there." She didn't want to give Robbi another opening to start in on the boy.

"Jason, over here," called someone.

The kids looked up to see Hayley, another one of the cheerleaders, waving in Jason's direction. She sat in the midst of a group of popular kids at a table in the center of the lunchroom. Jason glanced at Cleo and Robbi, who was already looking away.

"I guess we'll see you later," said Cleo uncomfortably.

"Yes," said Jason, slightly ill at ease himself, "'til later then."

"Hmmph," snorted Robbi, once the boy had left. "I don't know why we're bothering to help him. He obviously doesn't even want to be seen with us, which suits me just fine, I might add."

Cleo looked thoughtfully after the boy, but didn't say anything.

"Come on," said Robbi, pulling her friend to a side table, "let's eat. I'm starved."

After school, the two girls met outside the tall iron gates of Walton and went to buy ice cream cones.

Cleo ordered a single dip of mint chocolate chip in a plain cone, then asked, "How long do you think the game will last? I don't want to get there too early."

"What?" said Robbi. "We have to at least see the end of the game. We're playing St. John's. It'll be totally wild." She turned to the girl at the counter. "Triple dip cappuccino and cookies in a sugar cone with chocolate sprinkles, please."

"But it's stupid," said Cleo, "I mean, I've seen soccer on TV and it's just a bunch of guys bashing into each other."

"Yeah, you've got a point there," said Robbi, "but come on, we gotta show some school spirit. Besides, if you don't go, you'll never know how much fun you're missing." She licked around the edge of her cone, careful not to waste a single drop.

The girls strolled leisurely down Broadway toward Cleo's apartment to unload their bags and by the time they reached the building, Robbi had persuaded her friend to catch the last half of the game. They left their book bags in the lobby with the afternoon doorman, crossed the street, and entered Central Park.

Walking southeast toward the playing fields, they passed Tavern on the Green, the famous restaurant in the park that was the scene of numerous celebrity bashes and the end point of the New York Marathon. Last December, Cleo's mom and dad had taken her there for dinner and that night the restaurant had been a fairyland with the courtyard decked out in tiny white and blue lights. Silver ornaments the size of honeydew melons had dangled from the branches of every tree, while indoors, fragrant garlands festooned the walls and a huge Christmas tree, decorated with Victorian ornaments, practically filled the lobby.

On the soccer field, the girls found the game in full swing, with both sets of bleachers packed. Normally, soccer didn't have this much of a draw, but Walton and St. John's had been rivals since the 1850s and the matchup was the highlight of the soccer season. Cleo noticed that even Mrs. McMillan had put in an appearance at the game. The headmistress was standing on the side of the field chattering away with a spindly, dour-looking woman in a navy-blue pinstripe suit.

"Who's the lady with Mrs. McMillan?" Cleo asked Robbi.

"Mrs. Gilbert, the headmistress at St. John's. She's supposed to be really mean," said Robbi. "Come on, I see some seats at the top," and without even looking at the field, she screamed, "Go Walton!"

Cleo spotted Jason on the sidelines crouched down and firing away with his camera at the game as well as at the cheerleaders who were surrounding him. Cleo sighed and followed her friend up the bleachers.

As the two girls squished themselves into the top row Cleo couldn't help noticing that they weren't the only latecomers. Liz Cameron was picking her way up toward Charles Maxwell and Michael Payton who were seated a few rows below Cleo and Robbi.

The two boys made space for Liz, but as soon as she got there, she began whining. "Charles-y, have you looked at these bleachers? They're filthy. I mean, I couldn't possibly sit down on them. My dress would get all icky and you wouldn't want that, would you?''

Charles leaned over, snatched Michael's book bag, and plopped it on the seat next to him, ''Here, this'll keep you clean.''

Cleo was mesmerized. Liz Cameron definitely had a power over boys—a quality that made no sense at all to Cleo. No matter how obnoxious Liz was, the guys never seemed to care, and what's more, they fell all over themselves to do whatever she wanted.

Maybe it's something you have to be born with, thought Cleo as she watched Liz fawning all over Charles. The girl planted a small kiss on his cheek, then meticulously arranged her skirt around herself and primly sat on the bag. Then she turned to Charles and said, ''So, have we scored any home runs yet?''

Cleo rolled her eyes. Even she knew the term in soccer was goals.

''That's baseball, Liz,'' said Charles with a superior smile and he began a detailed description of the rules of the game.

Robbi leaned over and whispered to Cleo, ''Charles might as well explain the game to your rabbit.''

''Don't insult Phoebe that way,'' said Cleo with mock horror, ''she's much smarter than Liz.''

Liz's next attention-getting routine was to talk non-stop, distracting everyone within fifty yards of her seat. ''I really wish our team had prettier costumes,'' she said, ''and how come they're so dirty?''

''I don't know if I can sit this close to Baby Doll,'' Robbi moaned. ''I may be sick.''

''We don't exactly have a choice,'' said Cleo, looking around the crowded bleachers.

Just then Walton scored a goal, putting them one point ahead and Robbi was immediately on her feet, yelling loudly. A few minutes later, after both teams had scored once again, Cleo was standing and cheering with everyone else, caught up in the spirit of the game.

Both sides of the field were jumping up and down in a frenzy and a couple of times, Cleo had to grab Robbi's jacket to keep her friend from falling off the back of the bleachers.

"You're going to make me deaf with all your screaming, Rob," said Cleo.

"Hey, screaming's the best part of a game. Oh, no!" cried Robbi.

St John's had just scored again and now the game was tied. Both sides were going all out and not one person in the bleachers was sitting. The teams were evenly matched and it seemed that the game was headed into overtime, but with only five seconds left, Andy Monahan took a pass midfield, dribbled the ball to the goal, and scored the winning point for Walton.

As the final whistle blew, Walton's side of the bleachers went wild and kids flooded onto the field congratulating Andy and the rest of the team. After the cheers quieted, Cleo overheard Charles boasting to Liz, "This is nothing. Next week, you're going to hear major applause when I am declared El Presidente."

"You'd better be right about winning, Charles. I've already got the Christmas Dance completely planned out, and I've got a lot of ideas for the Spring Dance." Liz closed her eyes and sighed. "Can't you just see it in powder-pink and mint-green? And I was thinking of a butterfly theme.''

"Did you hear that?" Cleo whispered to Robbi. "If Charles gets elected we're doomed. Walton will be voted the most tasteless school in New York."

Robbi opened her mouth to reply, but to her surprise, nothing but the ghost of her voice emerged.

Cleo suppressed a laugh. "I can't believe it—Robbi Richards speechless. I told you you were yelling too much."

Robbi thunked herself back down on her seat. "Very funny," she mouthed, rubbing her throat.

Cleo pulled her friend to her feet, then down toward the field. "Let's find Jason. We've got some work to do."

Jason was by the Walton goalposts where he was the center of attention of a group of cheerleaders and soccer players, all anxious to land a picture in the yearbook. Spotting Cleo and Robbi, he said a little too loudly, "Well, now, I seem to be all out of film."

Cleo and Robbi were amazed as the crowd magically dispersed.

"Works every time," Jason said to the girls with a wink. "Smashing game though, wasn't it? I think I got a wicked shot of Andy Monahan scoring that last goal."

"I can't wait to see it," said Cleo, while Robbi stared at a treetop.

"I'm developing the film tomorrow, and if it comes out, I'll be sure to show it to you," said Jason. Just then Chandra appeared at his side.

"Jason," she said, "we're all going to The Pizza Palace to celebrate. Wanna come?"

The boy looked at Cleo and Robbi, then back to Chandra. "I'd love to," he said, "but I'm afraid I've already made plans. Perhaps another time."

Cleo allowed herself a faint smile as Chandra gave her a superficial glance. "Okay," said the cheerleader, "but if you change your mind, we'll be there for a while." The pretty brunette tossed her head before prancing off.

Jason looked down and started packing his camera in a black padded case. "Shall we walk a bit?" he asked.

The trio rambled north following a park bridle path. "I have to admit, I'm stumped," said Jason. "How do we stop Charles now? The only thing I can think of is to catch him in the act, but I haven't the faintest idea how to do that."

"Camcorder," whispered Robbi.

"What's happened to your voice?" Jason whispered back.

"Too much screaming," explained Cleo.

"Pity," said Jason, without a trace of sympathy.

"What do you think, Rob," asked Cleo, letting the comment pass, "could we really use your dad's camera?"

Robbi nodded vigorously.

"But how are we going to record those fellows at the crucial moment?" asked Jason.

"I've got it!" said Cleo. "What if we hide out in school until everyone's gone. Then we could set up the camera in Mrs. McMillan's office someplace where the Three Stooges won't see it.''

''I like it,'' said Jason. ''But are you certain there's a spot to hide a camera?''

Cleo fingered the locket around her neck before answering. ''I was in the office yesterday''—she shrugged—''there's shelves and books and lots of stuff in that room. I'm pretty sure we can find a hiding place.''

''We'd better *know*,'' said Jason, ''and that means checking out the office, preferably when it's empty.''

Cleo looked at Jason. ''Mrs. McMillan's office is never empty. She and Ms. Appleby are always there.''

''Every minute of the day?''

''Practically,'' said Cleo, ''and if they're not in, the door's locked. Maybe one of us will have to make up an excuse to go in and talk to her.''

''It'd be pretty hard to check out the room thoroughly if we're trying to talk to Mrs. McMillan,'' said Jason. ''Isn't there some other way?''

Robbi stopped walking and started digging in her backpack. After taking out a notebook and pen, she scribbled furiously and held up a piece of paper. WHAT ABOUT OPEN HOUSE?

Open House at Walton was not only for the parents of Walton students, but for parents who were considering sending their children to the school the following year. The evening was a bit of a madhouse with adults rushing around the building trying to decide in one evening if what Walton had to offer was right for their child.

Cleo thought about this. "I don't know. I mean, yeah, all the rooms will be open, and I'm sure we can even find a moment when Mrs. McMillan is out talking to parents, but how are we going to get into her office without being noticed?"

"It does seem quite risky," said Jason. "If we get caught, it'll be hard explaining our way out of it, and we'll be the ones in trouble, not Charles." He shook his head. "We may be better off chancing it Tuesday night."

Robbi's shoulders slumped in disappointment.

"Unfortunately," said Jason, "I may be a bit of a zombie on Tuesday. I've an appointment with the dentist to have a filling put in and they're sure to give me some sort of painkiller." He screwed up his face. "It's at the Columbia Medical Center with a Dr. Chiu who works with a lot of students. I do hope they're not going to experiment on me."

"Well, even if they do, I hope you'll be okay by eight o'clock that night," said Cleo. "If we can't stop Charles and Liz we'll be stuck with lollypop dances all year."

The thought sobered the trio as they walked to the edge of the park where Jason got on the M10 bus that took him uptown via Central Park West. When the two girls were alone, Robbi sat on the park stone wall and scrawled out another question. DO YOU REALLY THINK THE CAMERA TRICK WILL WORK?

Cleo wrinkled her brow as she sat next to her friend. "I don't know."

Robbi tore the old page out of the notebook, crinkled

it up in frustration, and started a new page. WAITING IS
DUMB. WHAT ELSE CAN WE DO?

"I can't think of anything, can you?" answered
Cleo. "And I'm going to be gone all weekend. Now I
almost wish I wasn't going."

The expression on Robbi's face was a sarcastic
"Yeah, right." She knew how much her friend was
looking forward to this particular trip.

Usually when Cleo's mother was working in Paris,
Cleo and her father went over to visit, but this time,
Mr. Oliver was too busy working on a story for *The
New York Times* Sunday supplement. This would be a
very special trip for Cleo because for the first time the
Olivers were going to let her fly overseas by herself.

"You know, the election's not until Tuesday," said
Cleo, "so we'll still have a little time after I get back
to find a way into Mrs. McMillan's office. Like Jason
said, we need to *know* that we can find a place to hide
the camera."

Robbi nodded and wrote, BUT HOW?

Cleo, deep in thought, watched an elegantly dressed
young couple get out of a taxi and go into a building
across the street. Suddenly she felt the rumblings of an
idea and she tapped her friend on the arm. "Listen,
Rob, do you think I could borrow some of your mom's
books?"

Robbi nodded automatically, then narrowed her eyes
and scribbled, WHAT KIND OF BOOKS?

Cleo was matter-of-fact as she stood and answered,
"Makeup? Costumes?"

Chapter 10

After retrieving Robbi's book bag from Cleo's lobby, the two girls walked uptown toward the Richardses' brownstone. Robbi was bursting with questions, dying to know what Cleo was up to, but without much of a voice, she could only communicate with her arms and her body. For seventeen blocks the small teenager orbited her friend, oblivious to the looks she was getting as she acted out an elaborate game of charades. By the time the girls reached the brownstone, Cleo was dizzy from watching Robbi try to make herself understood.

The Richardses lived in a skinny five-story town house crammed between two apartment buildings on 86th Street not far from the corner of Riverside Drive. New Yorkers called these structures brownstones, no matter what color they actually were, and Cleo liked the fact that the Richards house really was brown, except for a few splotches of colorful graffiti.

Inside, the girls picked their way up a newly installed winding staircase and climbed to the fourth floor. "Careful," whispered Robbi, pointing to the walls, "there are nails sticking out." Robbi's father was an architect who was renovating the brownstone in his spare time (of which he had very little). This meant there were always blobs of plaster or sprinkles of sawdust on the floor and the configuration of the house seemed to be changing constantly. The more work Mr. Richards did, the further away the place seemed to be from completion, but Cleo could see that when everything was finally done it was going to be a really fantastic home.

Robbi led the way to the fourth floor where she and her brother had bedrooms. Posters had been put up on the unpainted plaster drywalls in Robbi's room, but as yet, there wasn't even a door on the girl's closet. Robbi tossed her books on her bed and the girls headed back downstairs.

One of the few completed rooms was a library on the third floor. By combining two bedrooms, Robbi's father had created an ideal space for his family of book fiends and Mrs. Richards had furnished the space with large overstuffed chairs, lots of pillows, and floor-to-ceiling bookcases. This was no dingy, forbidding, traditional library, but a room that was decorated in cream colors and pale shades from nature. There were plush carpets on the floor for spreading out homework, and a window seat that overlooked 86th Street that was

without a problem, though she did have to stop every few steps to shift the bag from one hand to the other. It was already late when she got to her apartment and though she was anxious to start her reading, she realized she was also very hungry.

The aroma of Nortrud's beef Stroganoff hit Cleo the moment she stepped out of the elevator and as if on cue, her stomach growled loudly. She put down her heavy bag and as she hurriedly set the table, Cleo managed to sneak quite a few croutons from the housekeeper's salad.

"I saw that, missy," said Nortrud, swatting the girl away. "You go on and wash up. Dinner will be when your father comes home—whenever that is."

After snitching two carrot curls for Phoebe, Cleo carried the books to her room and began her "unrequired reading." Mr. Oliver didn't arrive for close to an hour and by that time Cleo had gotten a good start. She was so eager to try out some of the things she had learned that the moment she sat at the table she began wolfing down her food.

"Pretty hungry, huh?" asked Mr. Oliver.

"Uh, yeah," answered Cleo, swallowing her last mouthful of food. "Dad, can I be excused? I've got a lot of work to do."

"What is it? Something I can help you with?" offered Mr. Oliver.

"No, thanks," said Cleo. Whenever her dad "helped" with her homework, the assignments seemed to take twice as long to finish, because he insisted on digging up every possible, and often unnecessary, fact.

"Oh," said her father, looking slightly hurt, "okay."

Cleo looked at him, then quickly reconsidered her answer. "Actually, Dad, maybe you *can* help." She paused a moment, wanting to be sure she worded everything correctly. "I'm, ah, thinking about doing a paper for social studies on espionage, you know, spies, disguises, and all that. You wouldn't happen to have any information on that, would you?"

"Hmmmm, I don't know. I might," said Mr. Oliver teasingly.

"Dad, yes or no? I'm serious," said Cleo.

"I'm sure I have a thing or two," said her father with a smile. He was always happy when someone asked him for information he could provide. "But how about if we finish our dinner first, without trying to set an Olympic record for chewing?" Cleo had to force herself to sit still while her dad took a second helping.

After a slice of Nortrud's rhubarb pie (which was so good it made Cleo forget her hurry) Mr. Oliver led his daughter down the hall and into his home office—a room that Mrs. Oliver fondly described as "full of impending disaster." Books and magazines stood in piles waist high, and every available flat surface was covered with research materials and notes for Mr. Oliver's current project. Only the fax machine and computer keyboard were clearly visible.

"Let's see . . ." Mr. Oliver said, looking in the back of one of his sagging bookshelves. He had collected so many books over the years that they were stacked three deep on his shelves, some even stuffed in on their sides in an attempt to utilize every inch of free space.

Cleo cautiously lifted a few folders on her father's desk only to discover a dried apple core and two plum pits. "Eww, Dad. You're so gross," she said, dropping the folders back into place.

"Here they are," called Mr. Oliver, not even hearing his daughter. He waved several pamphlets and a thin book. "Remember when I did that article on double agents a couple of years ago? Good thing for you I never throw anything away."

Mr. Oliver, wearing his best self-congratulatory smile, passed the material to Cleo. She looked down and saw that what she held in her hand were several training manuals published by the FBI and the CIA. Across the first page of the pamphlets, stamped in large red letters, was the word "CLASSIFIED."

"Oh my gosh, Dad. This is great. Thanks." Cleo kissed her father and practically ran back to her bedroom.

Mr. Oliver called after her, "Don't show those to anyone else and be sure to give them back to me when you're done."

Cleo climbed into her cuddy chair and flipped on the brass stand lamp over her shoulder. A hundred years ago the lamp had burned whale oil, but it had been converted to electricity in the 1920s. Both the chair and lamp had once been in Cleo's grandmother's home in Maine before the woman had sold the house and moved to Florida.

The lamp and chair had been placed in a particular corner of Cleo's room so that she could sit and look out her window over the rooftops and penthouses of the Upper West Side. It was a view that on a clear day stretched farther than the George Washington Bridge, but Cleo had no time to appreciate the skyline this afternoon.

The second she opened one of her dad's pamphlets she knew she had struck gold. The pages were packed with detailed information meant for use by FBI and CIA operatives working undercover—character and age makeup, hairstyles that completely changed a person's look, ways to be inconspicuous in both urban and rural "situations," walk and posture hints, tips on making incredibly fast quick-changes, and info on how to use coats, hats, uniforms, and all kinds of clothing in the art of disguise.

Cleo was so fascinated that she stayed up far longer than she expected studying the CLASSIFIED manuals. At 4:00 A.M. she was still reluctant to turn off the light, but she knew she needed to pace herself. Tomorrow would be her last day at school and she wanted everything for the following week carefully planned out before she left for Paris.

Besides, thought Cleo as she snuggled into her grand bed and pulled the covers up around her long neck, *I've got to be on my feet next week for a "covert operation."* She had a possible plan in mind and, if everything went perfectly, Cleo thought she just might be able to pull it off.

Chapter 11

The next morning Cleo's alarm rousted her from a deep sleep. Still groggy, she hit the snooze button and caught a few more minutes, but after the alarm had gone off twice more, it began to register that this was going to be a very full day. She dragged herself out of bed, shuffled to the bathroom, and splashed cold water on her face. Slowly the fog began to clear.

After putting on a beige and coral tunic-length sweater with a large floral pattern and matching beige leggings, Cleo rushed to the kitchen. She gulped a glass of orange juice and grabbed her lunch bag, ready to run to the front door, but a stern look from Nortrud stopped the girl. She meekly walked back to the counter and picked up a freshly baked blueberry muffin that she wrapped in a paper towel to take with her.

''You don't have even five minutes to sit and digest

your breakfast?'' asked the housekeeper.

"No, I really don't,'' said Cleo. ''Honest, Nortrud, I promise I'll eat the muffin on the way to school.''

The woman did not look pleased, but placated herself by handing an extra muffin and a banana to Cleo. Satisfied her charge would be getting a nutritious meal, Nortrud accepted a peck on the cheek, then returned to putting the morning dishes in the dishwasher.

"And hurry home right after school,'' the woman said. ''We've got to get your bags packed, and you'll need to rest before you catch your flight.''

"Yes, Nortrud,'' said Cleo. She waved and headed out before the housekeeper could say another word.

Cleo arrived at school having eaten only one of the muffins. She stowed the rest of her eat-and-run breakfast in her locker, knowing it would make a great snack later on, and raced to homeroom.

She was dying to talk to Robbi about the plan for catching Charles and hoped that for once, her friend might show up in class a little early. But at 8:25, just before it was time to head on out to first period, Robbi scurried into the room. She waved to Mr. Gorgolo, the homeroom teacher, who merely nodded to the small girl and checked her name off his list. Then Robbi looked around for Cleo who was already heading her way.

"Come on,'' said Cleo. ''We've got to talk.''

The girls had three classes together and first-period math was one of them. Usually they had some time during this class to work on their assignments and get help from the teacher. A moderate amount of discussion, as long as it appeared to be about math, wouldn't be out of order.

Unfortunately, it was a day when their teacher launched into a whole new subject and talking became impossible. Cleo was burning to divulge her plan and began writing out her ideas on a scrap of paper.

YOU WERE RIGHT ABOUT OPEN HOUSE. I THINK WE CAN FIND OUT WHAT WE NEED, BUT I'LL HAVE TO GO IN ALONE. WHAT DO YOU THINK? read the note. Cleo folded the already small piece of paper into eighths. The moment the teacher turned to face the blackboard, the girl leaned over and tossed the note onto Robbi's desk.

Robbi read, her wide eyes and gaping mouth instantly telling Cleo she approved of the plan. Robbi scribbled on the back side of the note and waited for an appropriate time to throw it back to Cleo.

AWESOME! HOW ARE YOU GOING TO GET IN?

Cleo crumpled the note, stuck it in the side pocket of her pack, then started in on a new piece of paper. I'M GOING TO . . .

"Cleo?"

Cleo jerked her head up to see Dr. Smith looking straight at her. It was obvious from the tone of the teacher's voice that she had been asking Cleo something, but Cleo hadn't the slightest idea what it was.

"Yes, ma'am?" said Cleo, mortified to find everyone in the class staring at her.

"I asked if you understood everything so far. It appears that you were taking quite a lot of notes.'' Someone in the room giggled and Cleo felt her face turning red.

''I think I've got it all, Dr. Smith,'' the girl said, hoping the teacher wasn't going to walk over and look at her notebook.

Dr. Smith gave Cleo a questioning look, but said, ''All right, Cleo,'' before resuming her lecture. Robbi mouthed a ''whew,'' then motioned for Cleo to continue writing.

But Cleo was nervous now. Though she was dying to tell Robbi the rest of her plan, she didn't dare risk being caught again. She managed to pay close attention to the lecture for fifteen minutes, but when Dr. Smith turned back to the blackboard to write out a complicated equation, Cleo couldn't resist the temptation to finish the note she had begun earlier.

She pitched it lightly across the aisle to Robbi but, to her complete horror, she overthrew the note and it landed far beyond Robbi's desk, near the windows.

Robbi stuck out her foot, hoping to catch the paper under her toe and reel it in. She sunk down in her seat, stretching out with her toe pointed toward the white square, but without legs as long as Cleo's there was no way to reach it. Both girls' attention was riveted on the tiny wad of folded paper.

Robbi slid down in her chair as much as possible and had almost reached the note with her toe when suddenly a big shoe stepped down squarely on top of the little piece of paper. The girls saw the foot belonged to their worst nightmare—Charles Maxwell. He had been observing the note passing and, wanting to give the girls a hard time, had gotten out of his seat. He was standing by the window grinning at Cleo and Robbi, as the rest of the class, including the teacher, turned to watch.

"Excuse me, Dr. Smith," Charles said. "It's a little stuffy in here. I thought I'd open a window so we could all get some fresh air."

The teacher smiled at the boy. "Why thank you, Charles. That's very thoughtful of you."

Charles gave the teacher his most charming smile, then pushed up a window that was so old the glass was wavy. Then he bent over and swiftly scooped up the note. Cleo bit her lip as the boy taunted her with the paper.

The girl knew that one of the few things she and her friends had going for them was the fact that Charles didn't have an inkling they knew what he was up to. If he read her note, the cat would be out of the bag.

On his way back to his seat he leaned over Robbi's desk and dangled the note in front of Cleo, then snatched it away again. Cleo was in no mood for Charles's teasing, but she didn't dare get him mad either. She tried to smile as she whispered, "Please?"

Robbi wasn't as diplomatic. She poked Charles hard in the stomach and said, "Hand it over, Maxwell," as she tried to snatch the note. Charles pulled away, but Robbi grabbed his wrist and held on tightly.

Dr. Smith heard the struggle and her attention went to Robbi's desk. "What on earth is going on here?" she asked.

Charles straightened up and unfolded the small note. "I found this on the floor, Dr. Smith. I think Robbi was trying to help me stand up."

The teacher marched over to the boy, then stood, palm up, waiting for the note. Charles placed it in her hand.

"You may return to your seat, Charles," said the woman.

The boy smiled triumphantly at Robbi as he went back down in his seat.

"Is this yours, Robbi?" asked the teacher.

"It's mine, ma'am," answered Cleo, quickly speaking out. She didn't want to get Robbi in trouble for something she herself had started. Cleo could feel the teacher's eyes staring at her.

"Well, Cleo, I do not allow note-passing during my lectures. Unless of course it happens to concern the Pythagorean theorem." This got a nice laugh from the class, which pleased Dr. Smith to no end. "Is your note on the subject of mathematics?"

"No, ma'am," said Cleo, and she heard several kids in the class chuckle again.

"Then I won't bother to read it. But I will keep it on my desk. You can get it after class."

"Yes. Okay. Thank you. I mean, I'm sorry," stammered Cleo.

She forced herself to concentrate on the lecture for the rest of the class, but as soon as it was over, she rushed to the front of the room. Cleo smiled uneasily at Dr. Smith and stared down at the scrap of paper, which still sat in the middle of the teacher's blotter.

The math teacher picked up the note. "Would you like to tell me what was so important that it couldn't wait until after class?"

Cleo was torn. Here was her chance. She could tell Dr. Smith about Charles's plan and wash her own hands of the situation. It would be much easier if there was someone else to take charge of saving the election, but looking at Dr. Smith, Cleo knew it just wasn't a possibility. It would be the same questions about names and proof, and the teenager knew she would be doomed to failure again. Besides, she sensed her teacher was anxious to get to her next lecture and was only after a quick apology.

"I'm sorry, Dr. Smith. It's just that I'm going to Paris tonight to see my mother and I wanted to ask Robbi what clothes she thought I should take. I'm leaving right after school and, well, I'm sorry. I won't do it again. It was dumb." Her fingers snaked out tentatively toward the note.

"You're a good student, Cleo, so I'll overlook it this time," said the math teacher, handing the note back to the girl. Then she smiled. "Have a good time in Paris and be sure to go and see the stained-glass windows at Sainte-Chapelle if you have time. They're magnificent."

"I'll try, Dr. Smith. Thanks." Cleo pocketed the note and rushed out the door. It had been too close of a call.

Cleo waited until lunch before she revealed her plan to her friend.

"You're a total wacko, you know," Robbi said when she heard what Cleo had in mind, "but it sounds great." Robbi opened her lunch bag and pulled out an ultra healthy-looking salad. Before she could take a bite, she smiled and cried, "News flash! I just thought of something that might help. Remember I was a student volunteer last year? Well, at the beginning of Open House, the headmasters all gave a speech to the parents in the auditorium. It took about fifteen minutes."

Cleo stopped in midbite. *Of course,* she thought. *There has to be some sort of welcome and orientation. With luck, the school offices will be unlocked and I'll be able to slip in unnoticed.* Her plan to infiltrate Open House was definitely entering the realm of possibility. Cleo smiled and started chewing again.

The rest of the day sped by and in no time at all, Cleo and Robbi were at Walton's front gates saying good-bye. "Be sure you keep your eyes and ears open tomorrow," Cleo warned her friend. "I don't think Charles will make a move until next week, but you never know."

"Don't worry," said Robbi. "I've got the whole thing under control. You just have a good time and call me the second you get back, okay?"

"Definitely." Cleo grasped the strap of her backpack and headed for home. Jogging all the way there, she reached the apartment in minutes, just in time to see the "changing of the guard." The morning doorman's shift ended at 3:00, but the switch to the afternoon man could take place anytime between 2:45 and 3:30, depending on the two men's personal schedules. Cleo greeted both Max and Terry, before rushing upstairs where she went straight to her bedroom.

Nortrud had Cleo's suitcases already laid out on the bed—a pair of navy bags with matching bindings. Cleo packed the hanging garment bag carefully and efficiently, quickly pulling the clothes she would need from her closet and drawers.

She changed into comfortable traveling clothes—jeans and a baseball shirt with the logo of her favorite team, the Yankees. Next, Cleo sadly contemplated her feet, a wretched size nine, and decided her new white running shoes would be better for walking the streets of Paris than her red Keds. She tied her sneakers, then turned her attention to her carry-on bag.

Since she traveled regularly, Cleo kept the totebag permanently packed with her passport and a set of toiletries. All she had to do was put in whatever extras she needed, usually schoolbooks so she could keep up with her homework and a novel for the long periods she often spent waiting for her mother at fashion shows or photo shoots.

This time, in place of the mystery novels Cleo was addicted to, she packed the CLASSIFIED manuals her father had loaned her as well as one of Mrs. Richards's books on acting techniques.

When both bags were ready to go, Cleo picked them up and carried them to the front hall. Nortrud had set the teenager's plane ticket out on the small entry table and Cleo zipped it carefully into the side pocket of her totebag. From the coat closet, she pulled out her lightweight barn jacket with its big patch pockets and set it on top of her bags. After she had double-checked to be sure she had remembered everything, Cleo settled down to read the acting book while she waited for her father.

"All packed?" Nortrud asked, pushing the vacuum cleaner into the living room.

"Yep," said Cleo, "I think I'm ready." She curled her legs up onto the couch as the housekeeper plugged in the machine.

A moment later Mr. Oliver walked in the front door. That day he had made eleven stops all over Manhattan fact-gathering for his latest story and the man looked even more unraveled than usual.

"Ready?" he called, his voice booming over the vacuum cleaner. He picked up Cleo's bags.

"Wait a minute, Dad," Cleo yelled. She closed her book, ran to her father, and gently eased the suitcases out of his hands. She tucked her book into her carry-on, took her dad by the hand, and led him to the pantry area outside her bedroom.

Cleo's room was situated near the kitchen in what would have formerly been the maid's quarters. She had chosen it over the other bedroom (which her father now used as his office) in the hallway near her parents' master bedroom suite. Even though her room wasn't quite as large, Cleo loved the privacy, not to mention the fact that she had her very own bathroom.

"Dad, I just want to make sure you know how to take care of Phoebe," she said. Leaving her pet was the one part of traveling that Cleo disliked. Whenever possible, she took the rabbit with her and consequently Phoebe had seen more of the fifty states than most of Cleo's classmates. But going overseas there were almost always quarantine laws that made it impossible to bring along a pet. Usually when the Olivers went out of the country, Robbi looked after the rabbit, so this was the first time Cleo was entrusting the care of her precious "Bun" to her father.

"I've written everything down," Cleo said, handing her father a piece of notebook paper with careful instructions. "Phoebe's dry food is right here," she said, indicating a cupboard shelf. "She likes a little bit of bread in the morning and a carrot, but only the ones that are pure orange, no green or brown at the top. They're in a separate bag in the fridge. And, Dad, please, please don't forget to give her some 'petters' while I'm gone." Cleo knew her mini-lop thrived on affection as much as on the copious amounts of green pellets and vegetables she devoured each day.

Mr. Oliver was nodding his head, but looking off somewhere else and Cleo knew his mind was on another subject. "Dad!" she said. "Did you hear me?" She didn't understand why people always accused teenagers of not listening. Her father was worse than anyone she had ever seen.

"I got it," he answered quickly. "Food here, carrots in the fridge. Everything's written down for me." He waved the sheet of paper, then took it into the kitchen where he stuck it to the refrigerator with a magnet. "Come on, we'd better get a move on."

Cleo ran to the living room where she scooped up

the napping Phoebe. She gave her rabbit an extra special cuddle and said, "See you in a few days, Phoebe. I love you," and she kissed the bunny's nose and both of the big floppy ears before setting the beast back on the rug. "I'm leaving, Nortrud," Cleo called.

The roar of the vacuum cleaner stopped and the housekeeper came panting in from the Olivers' bedroom. "Okay, sweetie. Have a safe trip." She opened her arms and Cleo stepped in for a bear hug. "Did you remember to pack a sweater or jacket?"

"Yes, Nortrud." Cleo grinned and held up her jacket. "All set. Come on, Dad," she yelled. Mr. Oliver, taking advantage of the delay, had disappeared into his office and was busily clacking away on his keyboard. Cleo shook her head. She liked to be on time for everything, but it was very hard when she had to depend on her father to get her from place to place.

"Coming! Sorry, it just popped into my head how to lead off the article," he said, reaching for the garment bag. "Ready?"

Cleo put her carry-on over her shoulder and led the way out the front door. When the elevator arrived, she got in and waved a final good-bye to Nortrud who stood in the entry hall. The doors closed and Cleo sucked in her breath. Her weekend was about to begin.

Chapter 12

Terry, the doorman, grabbed the suitcases from Cleo and her father as they stepped into the lobby. "Off again, Mr. Oliver?" he asked as he followed the Olivers to their car.

"Not me this time," answered Cleo's dad. "Cleo's got a solo trip to see her mother."

"All alone? That ought to be exciting. Don't get into any trouble now, Miss Cleo," said the doorman. He loaded the bags into the Olivers' car that was double-parked just outside the green awning of the apartment building. Before they got in, Cleo's dad pushed a button on a small black device on his key chain, disarming the car alarm with a "boo peep" chirp. Holding on to a car in the Big Apple was not all that easy.

Mr. Oliver drove across to West End Avenue, then headed downtown toward the Lincoln Tunnel. Rush-hour traffic had already begun piling up, causing Cleo to glance at her watch more than a few times. Getting out of New York City was tough in the afternoons, and even worse on Thursdays and Fridays when Manhattanites escaped in droves to their country homes or weekend getaways.

The Lincoln Tunnel, which connected Manhattan and New Jersey, ran underneath the Hudson River and was one of the major arteries out of the city. As Cleo headed into the eerie, fluorescent-lit tunnel she felt like they were leaving civilization behind.

"Roll up your window," said Mr. Oliver soon after they joined a line of bumper-to-bumper traffic headed down beneath the bottom of the river. Here the trapped automobile fumes made breathing less than pleasant and Cleo cranked up the window, eyeing the walls and ceilings of the tunnel. Every time she went through she couldn't help wondering what would happen if there was a leak. Feeling silly, the girl put her hand to the roof of the car and thought, *Touch the ceiling in a tunnel, lift your feet over a bridge.* She knew it was only a goofy childhood superstition, but figured, *Hey, it couldn't hurt.*

After reaching the airport and checking in, Cleo looked at her watch and saw it was only a little after 6:00. Her flight didn't leave until 7:25 so they had a little time to kill.

"Want to grab a bite?" asked her father.

Cleo nodded. She knew she'd get dinner on the plane, but the meals were usually small and unappetizing. "A hot dog would taste great right now," said Cleo.

There were snack shops all over the airport and the Olivers found a small Nathan's stand not far from Cleo's departure gate. New York's own famous hot dog establishment had started as a single concession stand near the carnival rides of Coney Island and now there were restaurants all over the metropolitan area. Cleo ordered a chili cheese dog, fries, and a soda and her father got a sauerkraut dog, onion rings, and coffee. They carried their feasts to the side counters, sat on high airport bar stools that surrounded a small table, and dug in.

"See that man there?" whispered her dad. "The one in the plaid pants?" Cleo followed his nod and saw a balding man who also sported a butter-yellow polyester jacket and white patent leather loafers. He was glancing around furtively as he made his way past Nathan's.

"He's going to Florida to get in a weekend of golf," said Cleo, joining her father in his people-watching game. She and her dad would first pick someone walking by, then make up a whole story that fit with what that person looked like and what he or she was doing. "He's skipping work and planning to call in sick tomorrow from a golf course near Fort Lauderdale. And he hasn't even told his wife."

"Look at the way he's wiping his forehead and looking behind him," said Mr. Oliver. "He's especially nervous because he's just spotted his wife, who's picking up her best friends after a cruise to the Bahamas. She wanted to go with them, but her husband told her they couldn't afford it. If Mrs. 'Plaid Pants' spots him on his way to a solo vacation now, he'll be grounded for life.''

Cleo chuckled, but looked around at the crowd in the airport, as always curious to see what made people either blend in or stand out. She realized that the truant ''golfer's'' obvious jitters had drawn the eye even more than his garish, out-of-date clothing.

A woman dressed all in neutral colors walked past. Although she wore no makeup and had chosen drab, muted tones for her outfit, it was hard *not* to notice her. The woman had an aura of confidence in her walk and bearing that was so strong, half of the people she passed turned to stare, if only for a moment. Cleo wondered if the lady was someone famous who was trying to go incognito, but didn't realize her attitude would have shown through any kind of disguise. Cleo filed that thought away in the back of her head as she continued munching her hot dog.

It wasn't long before they announced Cleo's flight was ready for boarding. She hugged her father goodbye and couldn't help feeling a little nervous as she walked all alone down the ramp to the plane. Once inside, the flight attendants took care of Cleo, leading her to her seat and giving her a blanket and pillow for the long flight ahead. Cleo buckled her seat belt and settled in.

Twenty minutes later, as she looked out the window, the plane began taxiing out onto the field. Cleo clutched the armrest as the 747 sped down the runway, waiting for that moment when the plane became airborne, all at once the best and worst part of flying. As they soared skyward above New York City, her stomach did a small somersault and Cleo let out a small gasp of excitement. She looked for her apartment, but in a matter of seconds, the city was too far away and the dusky half-light of the hour blurred everything. A few lights twinkled below, but in only a minute the plane had left Manhattan behind and was flying high over the Atlantic Ocean.

Cleo wiggled herself into a comfortable position, pulled a book out of her carry-on, and opened it to a chapter on acting exercises that included improvisation—staying in character while reacting to any situation. *Wow, that's just what I was trying to do when I was at The Pizza Place,* thought Cleo.

She declined dinner and had been reading for about forty-five minutes when the flight attendant announced that the movie would begin shortly. Setting her book down, Cleo noticed it was already pitch-black outside. She decided she would rest her eyes for just a second. After all, she had been up very late the night before.

The next thing Cleo knew, she was being shaken lightly. A woman in an airline uniform was leaning over her saying, "We're about to land, honey. I need you to raise your seat back, okay?"

Cleo rubbed her eyes and looked around. It was daylight. She checked her watch and saw it said 2:15, but the six-hour time difference meant that in France it was actually 8:15 in the morning. Cleo pushed the button on her armrest and the seat back popped upright. In just a few minutes she'd be landing in Orly Airport and seeing her mom.

Mom. Cleo suddenly realized how much she had missed her mother. Though Alexa traveled fairly regularly, she left much more than an empty place at the dinner table whenever she was away. Mrs. Oliver was an optimist with a bright disposition, and what was remarkable was that she could make almost everyone around her feel the same way. Mr. Oliver liked to say his wife "had sunlight in her smile" and Cleo believed he was right.

The landing was smooth and Cleo clasped her hands anxiously as she waited for the plane to taxi to a stop. When it did, Cleo unbuckled her seat belt, pulled out her bag from under the seat in front of her, then shuffled along with the rest of the passengers into the airport.

"*Bonjour*, Paris," Cleo said under her breath, her fatigue forgotten in the excitement of being back in this beautiful city. Quickly, she got into the line to pass through immigration.

A short, but ramrod-postured man in a policemanlike uniform took Cleo's passport and flipped it open to her photograph. He studied the picture, then stared up at the girl's face. His short bushy mustache made him look a little like Charlie Chaplin and it wiggled with a life of its own when he spoke. "You travel a lot, mademoiselle," he said with a heavy accent and a demanding tone.

"Yes, sir," said Cleo, suddenly worried that for some reason she wouldn't be allowed into the country.

"What is the purpose of your visit?"

"To see my mother."

"Then your purpose is pleasure and not business?"

"Yes, sir."

Then there was a long pause while he wrote something on a piece of paper in front of him.

Finally Cleo couldn't bear to wait any longer. "Is there some kind of problem, sir?"

He glanced up at her sternly, obviously not pleased to have been interrupted. Then he opened her passport and said, "There is no problem whatsoever," and he stamped it with a flourish and handed it back to Cleo. "Welcome to Paris, mademoiselle. Enjoy your visit."

Cleo smiled with relief and the moment she stepped away from the man's booth she hurried to the baggage carousel.

Half an hour later, after she'd retrieved her garment bag and passed through customs, she began looking anxiously for her mother. Alexa was usually easy to spot in a crowd. Besides her height, there was that "sunshine" thing that always drew attention.

At first there were several other passengers waiting with her but before long, Cleo was the only person left from her flight. Then she heard an announcement over the loudspeaker, "Mademoiselle Cleo Oliver. Mademoiselle Cleo Oliver, *allez à le blanc téléphone.*" Cleo understood enough French to know she was being paged to go to a white telephone.

Chapter 13

Cleo looked around and found the nearest courtesy phone. She hoped whoever was calling would be able to speak English, because her own French wasn't quite good enough for most telephone conversations.

"*Allô?*" she said tentatively. When an operator answered, Cleo said, "*C'est Cleo Oliver,*" and hoped that would be enough.

"*Un instant,*" replied the operator before connecting Cleo to another line.

"Cleo?" came Mrs. Oliver's voice. "It's me. I'm sorry, sweetheart, but I'm caught in traffic. I'd forgotten how awful rush hour always is, but I should be there in a few minutes." Cleo could hear the car horns beeping and knew her mom was calling from a cab. .

"Are you okay waiting for a few minutes?" asked her mother.

"Sure, Mom," Cleo answered. "I'll be by the taxi stand."

"Okay, honey. See you soon."

Cleo went out to the curbside that was full of waiting cabs. French taxis came in all different colors and makes of car, but one thing they had in common was a loyal and friendly dog perched in the front passenger seat. They were all patient animals, most of no particular breed, who were quite content to while away the hours in the company of their beloved taxi driver masters.

Cleo shook her head "no" every time a taxi driver approached her, plunked her bags down on the curb, and sat on the garment bag. She had just taken out a book and started to read when she heard her name.

"Cleo!" Looking up, she saw her mother waving madly from an approaching taxi. The car drove up beside Cleo who was so relieved to see her mom, she almost started crying. After a bone-crushing hug, the two put the bags in the trunk and in moments they were speeding toward the city of Paris.

"You must be hungry," said Mrs. Oliver. "Are you up for a late breakfast at Carette's?"

Cleo nodded vigorously. One thing she always looked forward to when she was in France was breakfast. Although it was an unworthy meal as far as the French were concerned, it was the only time Cleo was allowed to have coffee. For Cleo, café au lait, served steaming hot in a cereal-sized bowl, was more than a beverage, it was a celebration. Not meant to be gulped on the run like American coffee, the bowl of half milk/

half coffee was best when savored over a leisurely hour at a sidewalk café.

They stopped by the hotel and dropped off Cleo's bags, then Mrs. Oliver gave the driver the address of Carette. The man nodded, grabbed a map, and unfolded it, then tromped on the gas pedal so hard that both Cleo and her mother were shot backward in their seats.

The taxi driver's maneuvers were more appropriate for the Indianapolis 500 than the congested streets of Paris, but the German shepherd in the front seat rode with his head calmly hanging out of the front passenger window, completely unperturbed by the wild ride. Cleo clung to the armrest on the door, listening to the taxi's tires squeal around the street corners and hoping the café was close by. The driver barely paid attention to the road but instead kept his eyes glued to his map that he held over the steering wheel as he tried to figure out the best back-street route for avoiding the rush-hour traffic.

"He's almost as bad as a New York cabdriver," whispered Cleo.

"Almost," her mother agreed solemnly.

Through some miracle, they arrived safely, though Cleo had the feeling a part of her stomach had been left behind at Orly Airport.

Carette was one of the Olivers' favorite cafés and they stopped in often during their Paris visits. The waitress knew Alexa and led her and Cleo to a great table on a terrace with an awesome view of the Eiffel Tower. Cleo looked around, unable to decide what was more interesting—the amazing Tower against the backdrop of Paris, or the fashionably dressed young men and women who frequented the café, often staying from morning to evening. The French loved to converse and Carette was the perfect site for lively discussions and debates on any subject from love to the cinema.

The Olivers, however, came for the food, especially the pastries. For instance, no lunch would be complete without having one of Carette's famous macaroons for dessert—a big meringue cookie sandwich filled with butter cream. For breakfast, the croissants were infamous and Cleo and her mom ordered two apiece.

"I'm so glad you could come," said Alexa. "It's hard for me to be away from home for more than a few days and it really helps when you can visit."

"Hey, Mom, it's not like I'm complaining."

"I guess not," said Alexa with a smile. "Listen, I've got the runway show today and a two-hour shoot tomorrow morning, but the rest of the time is ours."

"Great," said Cleo. "Maybe this time we can take one of the tours that's *above* ground."

The last time the family had been in Paris, Mr. Oliver had insisted on taking Cleo to see the catacombs, which had turned out to be pretty interesting, despite seeing so many bones and skulls. That would have been pretty tolerable, but Cleo's dad had also talked her into a tour of the Paris sewer system. Though it was certainly one of the most memorable tours Cleo had taken in Paris, or anywhere else for that matter, it was definitely not one of her favorites. Leave it to her dad to pick something really weird.

Cleo cradled her bowl of coffee in two hands and

sipped it as she watched the passersbys on the boulevard below. It seemed that every woman in Paris had a unique sense of style. Rich or poor, old or young, every one of them looked great and what's more, they knew it.

"What are you up for this morning?" asked Mrs. Oliver. "I can drop you back at the hotel or if you like, you're more than welcome to come along to the fashion show. Actually, I think you might enjoy this one. It's for charity, a joint effort of five different designers, if you can imagine that."

"Yeah, I'd like to go," said Cleo. Fashion shows were almost always fun, and watching from backstage was like going to the circus because everything was so hectic.

After breakfast, Cleo and her mom walked to the nearest métro station and caught the RER train, a superfast subway, which sped them in relative quiet to the Luxembourg Gardens where the fashion show was being held outdoors.

The gardens, Jardins du Luxembourg, had originally been created as the grounds for the Palais du Luxembourg, a palace that now housed the French Senate. Although the building was closed to the public, the gardens, spanning sixty acres, made up the largest city park on Paris's Left Bank, and a huge section of it had evolved into a playground for children with a carousel, donkey rides, sandboxes, even a pond for toy sailboats. It was here that a lavish white tent with a portable runway had been erected for the fashion show.

"Alexa, over here, *ma chérie*," called a short, pear-shaped man. He was peeking out from the entrance flap of a smaller tent that had been set up with makeup tables and changing rooms for the models. Cleo was amused to see that the man was actually wearing a beret.

"Darling," he said to Alexa, "I need a willing victim so I can show my assistants the face I'm after today, and you're the only one who's bothered to be here on time." Cleo thought there was something about the man's French accent that seemed not quite right, yet oddly familiar.

Mrs. Oliver answered the man, "Be right there, Jean-Luc." Then turning to her daughter she said, "Will you be all right?"

"Sure, Mom," said Cleo. The teenager had had lots of experience entertaining herself while her parents took care of business. She found a folding chair near the makeup tent and pulled one of the books from her totebag.

"Cleo, is that you? My gosh, you've grown." A beautiful blond woman stood looking down at Cleo.

"Hi, Juliette," said Cleo and out of habit, she immediately slouched a little.

"You're going to be as tall as I am soon," said the model.

Cleo cringed at the thought as she tucked her feet underneath herself to sit cross-legged. Juliette was six feet tall.

Other models began showing up in groups, some chattering in French, others in Italian or Spanish as they waited for their turns at the makeup and hair tables.

The next time Jean-Luc popped his head out of the tent he was looking at sixty of the most beautiful faces in the world.

"*Mon Dieu,* how will I get all of you painted with only three assistants?" he asked. "Well, let's get moving. You four, in here. And you there, the one who came in with Alexa, you're next."

Jean-Luc ducked back inside the tent before Cleo could say a word so she followed the four other women in and went over to his table.

"Excuse me, sir, I'm not, um, I'm not working," Cleo stammered. "I'm her daughter." She pointed to her mother who was nearby talking to a well-known designer.

"Not a model? Are you doing anything else?"

Cleo shook her head no.

"Well, now you are," continued Jean-Luc. "Two of my assistants haven't shown up and I need you to fill in."

"But I don't know what to do," said Cleo.

"Can you follow directions?"

"Yes," said Cleo.

"Then you know what to do. You're hired," said the plump little man. "What's your name?"

"Cleo."

"I'm Jean-Luc. No breaks until the show's over. Come here," he said. Taking hold of Cleo's hand, he dragged her to a specially lit chair in front of a makeup table. Though the girl felt a few flutters in her stomach, she couldn't help thinking, *This might actually be a lot of fun.* She'd never been asked to do anything before, except of course to stay out of the way.

"Stand here. These are brushes and these are sponges. You just hand them to me when I ask and put them back exactly where you got them when I'm done," said Jean-Luc. He checked his list and saw that Juliette, who was sitting in front of him, was in the first group of models who needed only light, almost imperceptible makeup. "Foundation sponge, second from the left," he said to Cleo, pointing with his chin as he fastened the model's hair away from her face.

Cleo picked up the small sea sponge and gave it to the man. "You must always begin with a clean palette," he said. "You'll never get a perfect finish if you have an imperfect start." Jean-Luc chose two foundations and deftly mixed them together just like a painter would mix his oils, until he produced exactly the right shade to match the model's skin tone. The man dabbed the makeup on lightly with the sponge until Juliette's skin appeared flawless. But Cleo also noticed that the model now had a very strange look, as if the definition and shape of her face had been smoothed away under the foundation.

He handed the sponge back to Cleo who placed it where she had picked it up. "You see how flat her face looks?"

Cleo nodded.

"Now, we put back the depth. Big brush on the left, and contouring powder," he demanded. Cleo gave the man what he asked for and watched as he masterfully sculpted a perfect nose, cheeks, and jawline.

Jean-Luc painted on the lightest of earth-tone eye

shadows and used just the lightest brush of mascara. A hint of pale pink lipstick was applied to Juliette's famous pouty lips and she was done.

"Magnificent, yes?" Jean-Luc asked Cleo, not really needing an answer.

Cleo wasn't sure she agreed with him. Jean-Luc had started with the nearly perfect beauty of Juliette, wiped it away with foundation, then had created virtually the same face. It seemed a contradiction to take so much makeup to look natural.

Jean-Luc read Cleo's reaction. "These are the ones I call the 'no makeup' girls. The art is to paint them without anyone knowing, but to make sure the faces 'read' from the stage. Even the most beautiful of faces would wash out under those harsh lights."

A moment later another girl took the hot seat in front of Jean-Luc and he began all over again. Cleo watched as he chose and mixed colors and soon she was handing the makeup artist the proper sponges and brushes almost as soon as he asked for them. When she began anticipating his requests, the makeup man gave her a warm nod of approval.

Two girls later Jean-Luc said to Cleo, "I'm so far behind and there are still so many girls to paint." He gestured Cleo over to the unused makeup table next to his. "Why don't you start Anita for me? Use these," he said, picking out two particular shades of base.

Anita, a dark exotic Italian model, who had known Cleo since she was seven, had been watching Jean-Luc work and happily sat down in front of the teenager. "Putting you to work, huh, Cleo?" She smiled. "Let me pull my hair back for you.'' The model swept her hair back with a headband from the table, then closed her eyes, ready for Cleo to begin.

Wow, thought Cleo, *I can't believe he's actually letting me do this.* She picked up the bottles and poured a little of each in the palm of her hand, then mixed them together with her right forefinger. She took a clean sponge and applied the foundation smoothly over the model's face. When Cleo had finished, she turned to Jean-Luc.

''How's this?'' Cleo asked with trepidation.

''Très bien,'' he said, moving in front of Anita. Cleo watched as the makeup artist used some lighter-colored foundation to bring the model's deep-set eyes forward just a touch before defining them with the peach shadows Cleo set out in front of him.

Working side by side with the makeup man, the teenager put foundation on another model, then ''graduated'' to helping with the finishing touches. Soon the girls in this first ''no makeup'' group were done and Jean-Luc and Cleo started in on the next bunch of models.

This time the makeup was vampire dramatic—dark red lipsticks and heavy charcoal shadows. Cleo learned to apply false eyelashes and found she was even able to alter the shape of the girls' eyes, from a round wide-eyed look to a hooded and very sexy look, by the way she positioned the lashes. The other three makeup styles that afternoon included a fantasy Star Trek-type makeup, a pale Louis XIV look, and a ''club'' makeup with black lips, white skin, and trashed eyes. By the time Jean-Luc, Cleo, and the other two assistants finished the last model, four hours had gone by.

Cleo's arms and feet ached but she was smiling. The teenager had just received, free of charge, an intensive hands-on lesson in the art of makeup. Suddenly everything she had been reading about in her cache of disguise books came together and made far more sense.

"Well done, everyone. Especially you, little one," Jean-Luc said, looking over at Cleo who beamed. It had been a long time since anyone had called her "little." "I never could have done it without you. Anytime you come with Maman, I will be honored to put you to work."

"Thanks," said Cleo. A question popped into her head and before she could stop it, it was out of her mouth. "Can I ask you where you're from?" Cleo still hadn't placed Jean-Luc's unusual accent.

The man narrowed his eyes, then burst out laughing. "You caught me," he said, dropping his pseudo-French accent. He leaned in close before spilling his secret. "Born and raised in Hoboken, New Jersey, as, get this, Joseph Benjamin Schwartz." He shrugged. "Hey, 'Jean-Luc' fit the image of a makeup artist a lot better so I changed it, but to my family I'm still 'Little Joey.' "

Cleo laughed along with the man. Now it made sense. What she had heard, beneath Jean-Luc's not-so-great rendition of a French accent, was a familiar, down-home New Jersey boy.

"Everyone knows," said the man, "but it's still fun for me to pretend that I'm a little more '*exotique*.' "

He gave Cleo a pat on the shoulder, then rushed off to powder and touch up the models.

Cleo looked around for her mother, but Alexa was nowhere in sight so the teenager went in search of an inconspicuous spot to watch the show. Her mind was reeling with the techniques and tricks she had mastered and she wanted a chance to write it all down before she forgot. She found a corner out of the way of the bustle of models changing clothes and designers screaming at assistants, took out her journal, and began jotting notes.

She noticed her last entry and thoughts of Charles Maxwell and the election came flooding back. Cleo smiled to herself as she considered her plan to infiltrate Walton's Open House next week. If she had a chance to practice what she'd learned today, Cleo was pretty sure she could pull off her ''covert operation.''

The fashion show had been a smashing success, attended by an elite crowd of politicians, billionaires, and even royalty. By the time the event was over, six million francs (about one million U.S. dollars) had been raised to build a children's hospital.

Since they were both exhausted, Cleo and her mom considered eating at a small restaurant near the hotel, but after a short rest, Mrs. Oliver decided to take her daughter out for a special dinner. The Jules Verne restaurant was nestled high on the second platform of the Eiffel Tower, 410 feet from the ground. Its black and gray decor was somewhat cavernlike, but nevertheless, a perfect complement to the fabulous skyline views.

"This is great," said Cleo, straining to look all around herself. *No wonder it's called the City of Lights*, she thought. Paris at night was a wonderland of sparkle—if possible, even more beautiful than Paris by day. Cleo found the view so breathtaking that she had to be reminded to pick out what she wanted to eat.

"Jean-Luc told me you were a big help today," said her mom when they were halfway through their first course. "He was very impressed with you."

"Yeah, well, it was fun," said Cleo. "And the show was great."

"Thanks for helping to make it a success. I'm really proud of you." Mrs Oliver smiled at her daughter. "How was school this week?"

"Okay, I guess." Cleo took a bite of her dinner, wondering if she should tell her mother about the election scheme. "Mom . . . ?"

"Yes?"

"If you knew someone was going to do something wrong, like, say, cheat on a test, what would you do?"

Mrs. Oliver's fork stopped halfway to her mouth, then she put it back down. "Well, I think I would probably tell someone in a position of authority, maybe a teacher. Why do you ask, Cleo? Is there something you want to tell me?"

"No," answered Cleo. "Robbi and I were just talking about it and I wondered what you thought." Cleo thought she sounded pretty convincing.

One thing about her mom was that she never pried too much. In a way, it was nice, but there were times Cleo wished her mother would be more of a . . . well, a mother, the kind who would ask a few more questions about what was going on.

Cleo knew her friends thought it was great how her mom treated her like a friend and never interfered, but sometimes the thirteen-year-old felt like she had too much responsibility. Most of the time it was okay, in fact, most of the time it was terrific, but every once in a while she really wished her mom would be there to take care of her and tell her what to do. Like now. She was aching to tell her mother about what was going on with Jason and the election, but when Mrs. Oliver started commenting on the view again, Cleo found herself unable to bring up the situation at school. This was a problem she would have to solve herself.

After a long leisurely dinner and a stroll along the Seine, they arrived back at their hotel that was only steps from the Luxembourg Gardens. The rooms were very small in comparison to American luxury hotels, but the Olivers loved the homey ambiance of the place and whenever possible, they reserved a room with a balcony. Another plus of the hotel was that the owners were always on hand to launch into a story about the history of the antique furnishings or to recommend the perfect café for lunch.

Cleo was very glad to be able to crawl between wonderfully fresh Italian sheets of a tall four-poster bed. But although she was thoroughly exhausted, the events of the day had her so keyed up that sleep was a long time in coming.

Chapter 14

The next morning Alexa was up early, washing her face for the day's magazine photo shoot. The sound of running water woke Cleo, but it wasn't easy opening her eyes. It always seemed to be hard for her to get out of bed the first day after traveling to a different time zone. Cleo was stiff from her ordeal the day before and it took a lot of effort to sling her legs over the side of the bed and sit up.

"Morning," she said groggily.

"Why don't you sleep a little more?" suggested her mother.

"No, I'm okay. As long as you promise we'll go have breakfast ASAP."

Mrs. Oliver laughed. "I should have known. You and your café au laits."

• • •

Over *"pain au chocolates,"* croissants filled with luscious lumps of melted dark chocolate, Cleo made the decision not to accompany her mother to the photo session. The shoots were often tedious and besides, Cleo had plans. That morning she had realized that Paris was the perfect place for a trial run of "Operation Open House," as Cleo had dubbed her intended masquerade. She wasn't likely to run into anyone she knew, which left her free to completely let go when it came to her disguise.

After they said good-bye at a métro stop, Cleo went back to the hotel room where she spread out her mother's makeup over the top of a small dresser. She banded her hair into a ponytail, picked up a hand mirror, and studied her face from all angles. Then she went to work. Even with everything she had learned the day before, it still took over an hour to paint her own face, but when she finally stepped back to look in the mirror, Cleo knew she was absolutely on the right track.

The teenager, in a wild moment, had decided to maximize everything about her features—accentuating her cheekbones, widening her already full lips and large eyes, darkening her thick eyebrows. Though she half expected to see a circus clown in her mirror, Cleo had applied her makeup so artfully that instead staring back at her was a striking and definitely interesting woman. By playing up the features she had thought were goofy, Cleo had actually drawn attention away from them—it was her face as a whole that was mesmerizing, and quite beautiful now.

She pulled one of her mother's crisp white linen shirts from a cedar-lined wardrobe and put it on. After rolling the sleeve cuffs up twice, Cleo tucked the shirt into a pair of her own jeans. Then she added a gold chain belt and a strand of her mother's fake pearls. Leaning over at the waist, she brushed out her hair vigorously.

When she stood up again, her hair was magnificently unruly. Cleo put her mother's Chanel purse over her shoulder, remembering to stuff a few francs in her jeans pocket. Pickpockets kept very busy in Paris and Cleo never carried money in her bag. She then walked around the room, posing and changing her walk in various ways until she had layered on a healthy dose of "attitude." Before leaving the room, she laughed and blew a kiss to her reflection in the full-length mirror by the door.

Cleo had decided that if she could be taken seriously as a customer in one of the expensive boutiques, she would have a good chance of pulling off her disguise anywhere. On a prior trip, while waiting for her mother to finish a long fitting session, Cleo had wandered in and out of some boutiques on the Right Bank of Paris. In every shop, Cleo had either been ignored or chased out, but this time she was determined to be treated like a potential customer. Though the couture shops of the Paris designers were across the river, there were plenty of places here on the Left Bank where she could test the effectiveness of her disguise.

Cleo sauntered toward the shopping area of Boulevard Saint-Germain in search of some unwitting "victims." Along a side street, she found a treasure trove of shops. As her first stop, she picked out a classy-looking boutique that carried designer labels from around the world.

Cleo let out a deep breath and shimmied her shoulders

in an effort to relax before approaching the front door. She walked to the center of the store and waited.

No response.

Cleo waited a little longer.

Still no response.

Cleo realized that she might look like a rich customer but she wasn't behaving like one. She immediately looked at her watch and began to pace impatiently.

Within seconds a saleslady sidled up to Cleo.

"Bonjour, madame. Puis-je vous être utile?" she said, asking Cleo if she needed help.

Cleo was overjoyed. Her disguise was actually working. *"Oui, madame, mais je suis désolée, je ne parle pas bien Français."* It was the first phrase she had learned years ago, "I'm sorry but I don't speak French well." Contrary to what was said about the snobbishness of French people, Cleo had found that everyone was usually helpful if she at least made the effort to speak some of their language.

"Zat is all right, madame," said the saleswoman. "I speak English. May I show you anysing in particular?"

"Yes, thank you, madame," said Undercover Cleo, keeping her voice low-pitched and the pace of her speech casual. "I would like to see something for a cocktail party I can't get out of attending next week."

The woman smiled and led the girl away to the back of the boutique and picked out several dresses she thought would complement Cleo's figure and coloring.

"I think I'll try this one on," the teenager said, pointing to a chic black dress. Not in her wildest dreams would Cleo have ever picked this one out for herself, but in disguise as an adult who went to cocktail parties, why not?

The saleslady was delighted as Cleo had chosen one of the most expensive dresses in the store without a thought to cost. The lady pulled Cleo's size and brought it to the dressing room where the girl slipped into it, then came out to look at herself in the mirror.

The saleswoman nodded appreciatively. "You are very beautiful, madame." Though the high-priced boutique had drilled its employees never to coo unnecessarily (preferring to let the sophisticated merchandise do the job of selling), the lady couldn't resist stating the obvious. And Cleo did indeed look breathtakingly beautiful.

After admiring herself for a few minutes, Cleo realized it was time to take the dress off. Reluctantly she turned to the saleslady and said, "It's very lovely, but I don't think I should buy it without my husband seeing it first. Perhaps I could bring him by next week. Shall we say on Tuesday?" Undercover Cleo waited, anxious to see if the saleslady would catch her in this monumental lie. Cleo was not at all sure she looked old enough to have a husband.

But the woman didn't hesitate in the least. "But of course, madame," said the woman with a smile, and she took the dress, hung it up, and walked Cleo to the door so graciously that for a moment Cleo wondered if she had bought something without knowing it.

"Until Tuesday then, madame. Please ask for Danielle," said the woman.

The woman had believed the charade so completely that Cleo felt bad. She made a promise to herself that the next time she came to Paris she would come back to the shop and buy something from the nice saleslady.

Cleo knew her success meant one very important thing—she looked and acted mature enough to be able to spend lots of money. She hoped it meant she would be able to sneak into Open House Monday night.

The only problem Cleo could foresee was that most of Mrs. Oliver's makeup was here in Paris. Cleo wasn't sure what had been left back in New York to create her "adult" face. Maybe she would be able to borrow some of Robbi's mother's supplies.

Cleo checked her watch and realized it was almost time to meet her mother at the hotel, but before heading back, she made one more stop. Her sweet tooth was calling to her and she headed for Debaube & Gallais, a shop just off the Boulevard Saint-Germain, that was renowned for its fine chocolates. Cleo went in and bought three truffles—one to eat on the way home, one as a surprise for her mother, and one more, wrapped beautifully in a tiny silver box, as a gift for Robbi.

Cleo and her mother spent the rest of the afternoon sightseeing, being sure to take in the beautiful church of Sainte-Chapelle. Almost before she knew it, it was Sunday morning and Cleo's whirlwind visit was over.

"I wish you could stay for the rest of the week," said Mrs. Oliver. "But I suppose there's school."

Cleo looked up from over her open suitcase. "Yeah, and the student body elections are this week. I really don't want to miss them. But you'll be home next Saturday, right?"

"I sure will. Now try to get plenty of rest so that you're fresh for classes tomorrow."

"Don't worry, Mom. I'm pretty used to this travel stuff by now. I've had thirteen years of adjusting to jet lag."

The Olivers took Cleo's suitcases down to the lobby and were almost out the front door when one of the owners of the hotel called after them. "Mademoiselle Cleo, someone delivered this to the hotel this morning. For you." He handed her a large present, extravagantly wrapped in gold paper with several roses on top.

Cleo's eyes opened wide and she couldn't help grinning as she took the box. Who could be sending her a present? She looked over at her mother who wore a puzzled and slightly mortified expression.

"Read the card first," urged Mrs. Oliver.

Cleo opened the small envelope and removed the card. "For Cleo, a very special assistant. Thanks, Jean-Luc." She lifted her head in time to see her mother breathe a visible sigh of relief.

"Go ahead, you can open it," said Alexa.

Cleo ripped open the paper to find a finely crafted cherrywood box with a brass handle and matching corner guards. It was the size of a toolbox and must have weighed fifteen pounds.

"I think it's a compass case," said Mrs. Oliver, "probably from an old sailing ship."

Burning with curiosity, Cleo lifted the lid to find that the box was fully stocked with makeup.

Her jaw dropped in amazement. Everything she could have hoped for was there—brushes and sponges, foundations, eye shadows, and lipsticks in many colors, a few sets of false eyelashes, and even putty for adding shape to chins or noses.

A squeal of delight escaped Cleo's throat as she pored over the contents. "Can you believe this, Mom?" she asked, showing the box to her mother.

"It's wonderful," agreed Mrs. Oliver. "Not that you didn't work hard, but it was pretty terrific of Jean-Luc to put all that together for you. You'll have to send him a nice thank you note."

"Definitely," said Cleo. "And don't worry, I'm not planning to glob this all on for school tomorrow. But now I can practice for next time, in case Jean-Luc ever needs another assistant." *And,* Cleo thought to herself, *it's going to make "Operation Open House" a whole lot easier.*

As soon as Cleo had settled into her seat on the plane, she began concentrating on her plan to stop Charles Maxwell. Walking around Paris where she was sure not to know anyone was much easier than what she had in mind for getting into Mrs. McMillan's office.

Cleo spent most of the flight studying her acting book and by the time the plane set down in New York, she felt she had some understanding of what it took to create a believable character.

That night at home, the teenager studied the CIA and FBI manuals and though she knew she should be getting rested from the trip, she was too excited. Finally, sometime around one o'clock, she reached up to turn off the light switch. *Okay, I've done my "homework,"* she thought, *Undercover Cleo is ready to go to work.*

Chapter 15

It was Monday night and Open House was about to begin. Cleo had spent hours perfecting her makeup and thought she was completely convincing as Mrs. Gilbert, the headmistress from St. John's. She wore a conservative dark gray suit, oversize glasses with purple-tinted lenses, and, most importantly, a black wig with a white streak on the left side. Cleo had styled the wig in a severe bun at the top of her neck and was sure she could pass for the strange woman she had seen at the soccer game.

An attack of the jitters struck as she was sitting on the stage of the school auditorium and waiting to address the parents at Open House. Her impulse was to turn and forget the whole thing, but she had gotten this far and knew it was only a matter of minutes until she was free to run out and examine Mrs. McMillan's office. Hearing her introduction, Undercover Cleo stepped up to the podium to welcome the parents. She smiled at the crowd, but as she lowered her head to look at her notecards, her wig slipped down over her eyes. Mortified, she pushed it back up, but it was too late.

As she frantically tried to rearrange the wig on her head, Mrs. McMillan ran out on stage pointing and shrieking, "You're not Agatha Gilbert, you're Cleo Oliver!" Two security guards rushed out and grabbed her arms, then dragged her away toward a waiting paddy wagon.

"No!" cried Cleo. "No, no, no!"

"Cleo, darling, whatever is the matter? It's just me, Nortrud."

Cleo sat up, still half in her nightmare, to find herself in her own bed. Nortrud sat on Cleo's bed beside her, lightly shaking the teenager's shoulders.

"Oh, no," said Cleo, "what time is it?"

"Almost 7:30. You've overslept a bit, dear. I think the jet lag must be catching up with you. Better hurry or you'll be late for school." Nortrud glanced at the pamphlet at the top of the pile of books on Cleo's bed-side table. "Hmm," said the housekeeper as she read the title, "*Covert Surveillance Techniques in High Population Urban Environments*? Times sure have changed. Whatever happened to good old readin', 'riting, and 'rithmatic?"

Cleo jumped out of bed, picked up the books, and moved them onto her desk. "It's a special project, Nortrud."

The housekeeper eyed the girl suspiciously but let the subject drop. "Well, hurry it up. I won't have you leaving this house without breakfast."

"I'll be out in a minute," answered Cleo as she tore through her closet looking for the plaid skirt she'd planned on wearing.

At school, the halls were buzzing with excitement. It was Assembly Day, always cause for joy since every class was cut by five minutes, but today had the added heat of the school election that gave this assembly a special significance. This would be the last chance the candidates had to get on their soapboxes and drum up votes.

Who's going to come out on top, Jason or Charles? wondered Cleo. *And how will it affect "Operation Open House" later tonight?*

A little before 2:30, the middle school students began filing into the auditorium. Cleo had taken a few minutes to go to her locker right after class so she arrived to find every seat up front already taken. Disappointed, she started for the back, then saw Robbi waving frantically in her direction. Her friend had saved her a great place in the second row.

As Cleo picked her way toward Robbi, she went through clusters of kids carrying posters and banners in support of their favorite candidates. If the messages on the signs were any indication, the race for the office of president looked like a dead heat between Charles and Jason.

While Cleo listened to the various speeches, she

watched her schoolmates and their reactions and realized that even though this was supposed to be an election, it had become more of a popularity contest.
Friends were rooting for friends, no matter what the
candidates were actually saying, and the students who
had chosen to run seemed to be the "in" kids at school.

When Cleo thought about it, she had to admit she
wasn't much different from anybody else in the auditorium. After all, what was her own reason for voting
for Jason—was it just because he never made fun of
her like Charles Maxwell always did, or did she gen-
uinely think he would do the best job? Suddenly Cleo
found herself sitting up straighter, anxious to hear what
the last two speakers, the rival candidates for president,
really had to say.

Charles took the podium first. He grinned at the
audience and winked at a row of girls before starting
his speech.

"I'm Charles Maxwell, as everyone who's anyone
knows, and let's face reality here, I am the only vote
you're gonna need to cast. Why? Because I'm going to
give you the school year of your dreams." Charles
went into a laundry list of how he was going to make
things fantastic. "A longer lunch hour. And how about
more time after lunch for our activities meetings? After
all, why should we risk indigestion? I call for a
leisurely lunch, followed by some serious socializing
time!" he shouted to the crowd who roared back their
approval.

"That is so bogus," Robbi whispered to Cleo.

"And how would you like the option of being able

to go to The Pizza Palace and get something other than the same old cafeteria swill? I move for getting off campus at lunchtime.''

Again Charles had to wait until the crowd quieted before he continued, ''Lastly, I propose an across-the-board reduction in homework.''

The students went wild. ''We know that Walton always scores high on the national achievement tests, so why are we being punished? Why do we have to do so much work? We have earned the right to have less homework!'' He practically shouted to the cheers of the crowd.

Cleo and Robbi stared at each other, both their mouths open. Cleo noticed Mrs. McMillan was standing to the side of the stage shaking her head and becoming extremely red-faced.

''Right,'' commented Robbi. ''If Charles were the President of the United States he couldn't deliver those promises.''

Cleo looked around and was amazed that most of the students seemed enthralled by Charles's speech. *What could this guy possibly do or say that's more ridiculous?* she wondered. It didn't take long to find out.

Charles Maxwell had saved his best for last. On cue, his cohorts, Andy and Michael, popped out of their seats and ran up and down the aisles, tossing free chocolate bars to all the students.

''In conclusion,'' shouted Charles, ''a vote for me is a sweet deal!''

The applause was staggering as candy rained down on the kids. Robbi caught two chocolate bars and handed one to Cleo before opening hers and taking a bite.

Cleo accepted the candy, but couldn't bring herself to open and eat it. Somehow it seemed like a bribe.

Charles smiled and even took a few bows after his speech. He knew he had scored high marks. As the boy walked back to his seat on the stage, he smirked at Jason who had the final speech of the assembly.

Jason knew he faced an uphill battle and stood up slowly before making his way to the podium. Cleo thought he looked unusually downcast and defeated.

The boy introduced himself and started his prepared speech, but his first few sentences were lost, drowned out by the crackling of hundreds of candy wrappers. Cleo leaned forward, straining to hear him, but almost everyone else, including Robbi, was involved in eating their chocolate bars.

Suddenly Jason stopped talking completely. It was a good move on his part because the silence quickly caught the students' attention. Only after it had quieted to a muted din of munching chocolate did Jason let forth a dimpled smile.

"Thank you. I won't speak long, but I would like you to hear what I've got to say—although what I propose is rather modest. I must warn you that I am going to speak only about things that I believe I can accomplish, not just spout a bunch of empty promises."

The truth of Jason's words hit home with many of the middle schoolers. With a few sentences he had exposed the hollowness of Charles's speech.

"My platform is simply this," Jason continued, "to

help you and me, the student body, to help ourselves. I want to propose a student/community job board where parents and local businesses can advertise for part-time student employees. I believe this can be not only a way for us to earn some extra pocket money, but a way to help our community become a better place as well.''

The mere mention of money had the auditorium riveted to Jason's words.

''And perhaps a section of the job board could be set aside for student tutors so that we could help each other with classwork.''

Jason also expressed concern for the safety of Walton students, since several schoolmates had recently been harassed after school by other kids in the area. He proposed a buddy system and better cooperation with local police. He concluded with, ''The future is up to us. Let's make it what we deserve—the best.''

The applause for Jason's speech was nowhere near the applause that Charles had received, but the students seemed impressed and thoughtful. Cleo could hear many of her classmates talking about Jason's ideas as they left the auditorium.

''I have to admit,'' said Robbi, ''even though Jason's a jerk, he wasn't half bad up there.''

''Yeah, he was kinda good, huh?'' said Cleo. ''And he's not really being a jerk, Robbi, he's just sort of teasing you. Give him a chance, okay?''

Robbi snorted but didn't answer as she headed toward the front gates of school. ''Well, are you coming?'' she asked Cleo.

''Uh, you go ahead,'' said Cleo. ''I forgot

something." Her eyes watched Jason surrounded by well-wishers as he exited the auditorium.

Cleo followed the group up the winding staircase to the lockers and hung back at the end of the hallway, knowing Jason would pass her on the way out. She was hoping to get a moment alone with him so she could tell him how much she liked his speech.

But the group around Jason only grew larger and Cleo started feeling uncomfortable as she waited alone at the end of the hall. Strolling to the water fountain, she leaned over and took a very long sip.

Just then, a burst of laughter drew Cleo's attention to Chandra Fisher and her cheerleader friends who were gathered around a bank of lockers. As the gaggle of girls moved toward Cleo, she turned and took an even longer sip of water.

"I just can't wait until Friday night," declared Chandra. "Everyone's going to be at Jason's party."

"Well, everyone that matters," corrected Chandra's best friend, Hayley. "What are you going to wear?"

"I've got to get something new," answered Chandra. "I'm going to make sure Jason notices me."

"I don't think you have to worry, he definitely likes you," said Hayley.

"Really?" Chandra was so thrilled to hear this, she spun around and knocked into Cleo, pushing her face into the stream of water.

"Oof," spluttered Cleo and as she stood up and faced Chandra, water ran down her face and onto her blouse.

"Sorry about that," said the girl. "We were just

talking about Jason's party." She looked pointedly at Cleo and asked, "Are you going?"

"I, uh, don't think so," stammered Cleo as she wiped water off her face. "I'm kind of busy Friday."

The five cheerleaders exchanged glances, then broke into giggles, knowing full well Cleo hadn't been invited. As Cleo wiped the water off her face and clothes, she heard Hayley's shrill voice asking, "What is the giraffe girl's name again?" The cheerleaders made a beeline for Jason, quickly melting into the crowd around him.

Blinking away her tears and for once feeling very grateful to be unnoticed, Cleo slunk down the staircase and ran all the way home.

Chapter 16

Cleo couldn't even manage a fake smile for Terry the doorman when he greeted her at the front awning of the building. In fact, she barely saw him as she plowed through the lobby. *Why didn't I leave with Robbi?* she asked herself.

She dropped her books inside the front door with a satisfyingly loud crash, then clomped to her bedroom. After throwing herself across the bed and having a good cry, she raised her head and saw the books and manuals stacked on her desk. She stared at them for a moment, then went over and batted the whole pile onto the floor, determined to forget about the election and Jason.

Cleo had succeeded in working herself into a thoroughly bad mood when a soft knock on the door made her sit up and wipe her eyes. "Yeah?"

"It's Nortrud. Is anything the matter?"

"No," answered Cleo. "I'm fine."

"Good. Glad to hear it. Why don't you come out to the kitchen and help me unload the dishwasher. I could use some company," said the woman.

It was always hard to refuse Nortrud when she asked like that. "I'll be out in a minute," said Cleo. She heard a short grunt from the housekeeper as the woman turned and walked down the short corridor to the kitchen. Cleo took a moment to check her face in the mirror, making sure all her tears were gone before leaving her bedroom.

When Cleo stepped into the kitchen, Nortrud was just pulling some brownies out of the oven. "Just in time," the woman said. "Let's let the dishwasher wait while we have ourselves a taste test. Can't work on an empty stomach." Nortrud cut two large steaming squares, then poured a glass of milk for Cleo and a cup of coffee for herself. "Now, would you like to tell me why that bomb of schoolbooks landed in the foyer?"

Cleo took a large mouthful of the brownie in an effort to ignore the question, but the housekeeper was patient. After a third bite, the silence became excruciating and the teenager finally opened up. "There's this boy I've sort of been helping in the student body elections."

"A boy?" asked Nortrud.

"Yes, and I wanted to talk to him after the assembly today, but I couldn't get his attention. It's no big deal." Cleo took a sip of milk as she tried to decide how much to reveal. "I guess that's all," she said. It rang false and she knew Nortrud could hear it.

"Hmm"—the housekeeper nodded—"and I take it this boy is . . . special?"

Cleo lowered her eyes and then her head.

"Oh, honey," said Nortrud. "It's never easy, is it? I remember my first date when I came to this country. Did I ever tell you about that?"

Cleo shook her head. Relieved that she wouldn't have to divulge any more about the afternoon's events, she tucked her feet under herself and waited expectantly. Nortrud always had the most extraordinary stories.

"Well, I was only fifteen and my family had just moved to America. I'd studied English back in Austria, of course, but I certainly wasn't fluent yet. Still, I went to school here anyway and did my darnedest to understand everything that was being said.

"About a month after classes had started, when I'd gotten a little more familiar with the language and customs, I started noticing this boy in the halls. He always wore brand-new blue jeans rolled up at the cuffs— something that seemed so American to me. He had light brown hair, lots of freckles, and these sparkling blue eyes. Tommy Anderson was his name." The housekeeper sighed while Cleo looked on in amazement. She'd never thought of her beloved Nortrud as ever being young, let alone envisioned her as having had any sort of romantic life.

Nortrud took a sip of coffee before continuing. "Can you imagine how thrilled I was when, one day, the girl who sat next to me in math said that Tommy had been asking about me. She said she thought he wanted to ask me out. I know I didn't sleep a wink that night. I was far too busy playing scenes in my head of how the big moment would go.

"I waited all the next day and had just about given up when I saw him leaning against the wall outside of school," said Nortrud, giggling at the memory. *At least, it sounded like a giggle,* thought Cleo. It was a very bizarre sound coming from the housekeeper.

"Tommy stood up when I came closer and he fell into step with me. I was so excited, I could scarcely breathe and I was sure I would forget every bit of my English. After about three steps, Tommy stopped and turned to me."

Nortrud took a deep breath. Then bit into the brownie and chewed slowly. Then she took a sip of coffee.

"Nortrud! Tell me what happened?" demanded Cleo.

"Oh. Well, he asked me to a concert that weekend." The woman smiled. "I was in seventh heaven. I'd expected maybe a date at the soda shop, but the Philharmonic? I checked the newspaper to find that the bill was Mozart that weekend, which couldn't have been more perfect for my first American date.

"The rest of the week went slower than molasses, but finally it was Saturday. I spent the entire day getting ready. Sat in the bath for an hour, then slathered on rose milk lotion so my skin would feel silky and smell sweet. I didn't wear makeup yet, but for that night, my mother permitted me to put on a touch of pink lipstick and a bit of rouge. Then came the crowning touch.

"My mama had made the most beautiful gown for me when we were back in Austria. It was my first grown-up dress and was made out of pale pink tulle with a satin bodice. I looked just like a ballerina in it." Cleo could not imagine Nortrud ever looking anything like a ballerina, but felt it would be best not to mention the thought.

"Well, at last the doorbell rang. My father opened it and let Tommy in. Even though I had been ready for over an hour, I was upstairs waiting to make a grand entrance down the stairs.

"I descended slowly, expecting my handsome young man to be looking up at me awestruck. Instead, I heard the most outrageous laughter."

Nortrud blushed even as she was speaking. "Tommy was doubled over in hysterics. I looked down and there he was, dressed in a striped T-shirt and one of his many pairs of blue jeans! When he finally stopped laughing, he told me he was taking me to the park. I pointed out that he had said 'a concert,' and he told me he had planned to take me to a band concert being held in Central Park. It had never occurred to me that there would be more than one concert in a city, or that it could be an informal event.

"Oh, I was mortified, I tell you. I turned and ran back up the stairs. Even though I heard Tommy calling after me to change while he waited, I just couldn't bring myself to do it and finally he left without me. At school the next Monday, everyone knew, and though no one was really mean to me, I could hear the whispers and chuckles. I was horribly embarrassed and never did quite forgive Tommy Anderson.

"He asked me out one more time, but the damage had been done and not long after that, he started going out with a little redheaded girl." Nortrud looked out the window as she finished off her coffee.

"Anyway, after many years, I realized it wasn't anyone's fault, just a series of misunderstandings. But you know, I never forgot Tommy and that little redhead he eventually married. That might have something to do with me dying my hair red the moment I was old enough."

The housekeeper put a hand to her hair. "This isn't really my natural color you know," she said shyly. Of course, only half of the hair on Nortrud's head still showed any signs of her last visit to the beauty parlor and this time Cleo couldn't hold back her laughter. A guffaw exploded out of her and a moment later Nortrud joined in.

The two were wiping away their tears of laughter when Nortrud shrieked. "The pictures! I almost forgot. I swore to your father I'd take his film in today and the shop closes at six. Oh, dear, he said he needed them tomorrow and I promised . . ." The woman continued talking to herself as she grabbed her handbag and rushed out the front door.

Still chortling, Cleo emptied the dishwasher and put her dish and glass in before returning to her room. She realized her situation was similar to Nortrud's and no one was to blame for what had happened that afternoon at school. Jason hadn't done anything to hurt her and no matter how much she wanted to abandon the job she had started, she couldn't. She picked up the books from the floor (relieved to see that Phoebe hadn't nibbled on any of them) and arranged them neatly on the desk. There was still more work to do.

She chose one of the books and carried it to her cuddy chair, then it struck her that she was alone in the apartment. She set the book on the chair, then hurried to her parents' closet.

Taking advantage of the fact that Nortrud was away, Cleo began digging through her mother's clothes. She didn't think her mom would mind her borrowing an outfit or two as long as she was careful. Several dresses caught Cleo's eye and she put them aside to try on. Then she found it. Squished at the end of the rack, almost out of sight, was a trim blue businesslike suit with clean lines. It was perfect. Cleo pulled the outfit from its hiding place and held it up to herself for size. It had to fit.

Cleo couldn't remember ever seeing her mother wear this particular suit and checked to make sure it wasn't an expensive designer label. There was no need to borrow anything too costly when her mom had so much to choose from.

To Cleo's surprise, there was no label at all. The suit was made of an almost iridescent aquamarine silk shantung and though it didn't look exactly current, it didn't look out of fashion either. There seemed to be nothing special about the suit, but Cleo couldn't wait to see herself in it and scrambled out of her clothes to try it on.

It fit like a glove. Turning to admire herself in the mirror, Cleo was amazed to see that even the length seemed just right, at least for the purpose she had in mind. But now there was the problem of shoes.

Cleo went back to the closet and looked over the shoe rack that took up half a wall. The choices were dizzying, but she searched the rows of flats and found a pair in a neutral gray. On another shelf on the wall sat a handbag to match. Looking through the rest of the closet, she plucked a few more items from her mother's shelves.

On her way out of the room, Cleo stopped by Alexa's vanity to take a peek in her mom's earring bowl. The heavy cut-glass dish was one of Alexa's thrift store finds from an out-of-the-way shop in Maine.

When Mrs. Oliver had spotted it, the bowl was covered with several coats of paint and seemed completely unremarkable. Cleo and her father had not been impressed, but Alexa had given the store owner a dollar for the piece anyway.

Later she had cleaned it by hand and found that beneath the paint, the bowl was made of slightly yellowish glass. The rare type of glass called "Golden Glow" had been produced in very limited quantities during the Brilliant Period in the late 1800s.

Mrs. Oliver had placed the little condiment dish on her vanity so that when the morning sun hit the deeply cut facets, the bowl sparkled with a rainbow of brilliant colors. Cleo never tired of looking at either the splay of light coming from the wonderful dish or its contents—an eclectic assortment of Alexa's earrings, from kooky dimestore pairs to others set with wildly expensive jewels.

The girl's eyes were drawn to one particular pair of large gold and silver circles. She picked them up, then clipped them on, thankful the pair wasn't for pierced ears. Though Cleo had accompanied Robbi on three occasions when her friend had pierced an ear (she'd put three holes in her left ear and one in her right), Cleo still wasn't sure she wanted to have it done herself. She kind of liked her smooth earlobes and besides, no matter how much Robbi said it didn't hurt, the earring gun looked pretty vicious. And as for piercing a belly button like some of the models her mother worked with . . . well, it was too gross for words.

Cleo gathered the items she wanted and carried them to her bedroom. It was amazing but the aquamarine silk outfit had a life of its own, almost molding her body and somehow even changing the way she moved. Rather than her usual slouches, Cleo couldn't help but stand straighter and more "adult," which, she had to admit, was a lot more comfortable than trying to contort her body down into something shorter. After she was satisfied with her new "look," Cleo removed the outfit and hung it up carefully in her closet.

Half an hour later Nortrud was back in the kitchen, bustling about and putting last-minute touches on dinner, and Cleo's father was seated in the television room, reading a magazine and munching on a carrot.

"Dad, I hope that's not one of Phoebe's carrots," said Cleo.

"Phoebe's carrots? Did she pay for them?"

"Da-ad. Hers are in the Ziploc bag. Remember?" said Cleo.

Mr. Oliver rolled his eyes with a touch of guilt. "I might have taken one from the bag," he conceded. "But really, Cleo, I think the Bun could spare just one for me."

Cleo tried giving her father a stern look, but failed. "I guess it's okay this once. But next time double-check," she said. "Are you home for the night?"

Like many New Yorkers, the Olivers had a lot to do on week nights and it was rare that all three spent an entire evening together in their apartment. Alexa and Scott Oliver were invited to everything; a new exhibit at the Metropolitan Museum of Art, the opening night of a Broadway show, a charity ball for five hundred at the Plaza Hotel, a private screening of an unreleased film, or even dinner with Uncle Lionel at his favorite Chinatown restaurant.

The Olivers would have preferred to spend more time at home, but as Cleo's dad said, "Socializing is the foundation of any Manhattanite's job." Of course, if he was working on a project that had a deadline, Mr. Oliver would decline all invitations until he finished writing.

"I'm in tonight," Mr. Oliver said, "trying to wrap up the Jimmy Ray Tyson story. I've got the tedious job of listening to my interview tapes again. I have this gut feeling there's something in the facts I'm not seeing and I really want to nail this J.R.—he's a bad one."

"Can't you just look at your notes?" asked Cleo.

"Yeah, but since I've got to be sure, I need to compare them to my tapes. It's always a good idea to have a backup system. If you're not careful, you can write down what you want to hear, not what was actually said.''

"Really?" asked Cleo. "Have you ever done that?"

"You dare to ask your perfect father if he would ever commit an error in reporting?" Mr. Oliver feigned a shocked gasp.

Cleo laughed, but found herself thinking about what her father had said while she ate dinner later on. If only she had been able to record Charles's conversation with his friends at The Pizza Palace. Then she would have had all the proof she needed to convince Mrs. McMillan.

After the meal, Cleo excused herself and went to her room. She pulled out the makeup box Jean-Luc had given her and plunged in. Half an hour later, after careful preparation, she was ready for action. Carrying her shoes in her hand, she crept to the door and listened for the whereabouts of her father and Nortrud. The clicking of her father's keyboard and the clanking of the pots and dishes in the kitchen told Cleo her escape route was clear. Her stockinged feet tiptoed down the hall and she silently slipped out the front door of the apartment.

A young woman walking down Columbus Avenue paused to check her appearance in the window of a shoe store on 71st Street. She was pleased to see she looked properly chic with a chiffon scarf wrapped around her hair and neck, its ends tucked neatly into the jeweled neckline of her suit. Beneath the scarf, the lady's hair was lightly teased, giving her head some size and her slim frame even more height. *Not bad*, thought Cleo, admiring herself. *Not bad at all.*

She had done her homework well. The makeup job had been done skillfully and she had also added a few fine age lines around the corners of her eyes, forehead, and mouth.

One trick she had learned from the CIA manual was that hairline and hair color were fast, radical ways to change one's appearance, so Cleo had put on a blond wig borrowed from her mother. With the scarf concealing her thin youthful neck, and dark glasses adding a certain mysteriousness, the schoolgirl had been truly transformed.

Undercover Cleo, playing a prospective parent, walked through the front gates of Walton. The second she was in the courtyard she automatically began to hurry, as if she were going to class. Then she caught herself. Remembering that grown-ups and kids walk differently, Cleo stopped to study the measured steps of a tall woman coming toward her in the corridor. When Undercover Cleo started walking once again, she mimicked the older woman's gait perfectly, taming teenaged Cleo's high-energy bounce.

Almost every book Cleo had read said she needed to become a character totally, even think like the character if she was going to fool people. Now as she continued her methodical saunter, Undercover Cleo nodded coolly to the other parents.

A group of confused-looking adults were gathered around one of the student volunteers near the stairs. One particularly exasperated couple on the outskirts of the crowd had turned to look for another student guide when they noticed Cleo observing the situation with an amused expression on her face. After exchanging a look, the man and woman left their place in the group and rapidly approached Cleo.

The teenager's first inclination was to pretend she hadn't seen them coming and hurry off. She was looking around for a place to run and had taken two fast steps backward when she realized, *I'm supposed to be an adult.* Undercover Cleo stood her ground and put on a smile.

"Excuse me," said the man, "you look like you know what's going on here. Where in the world are we supposed to go for the start of this thing?"

A chuckle escaped from Cleo's lips—a mixture of nervousness and relief. This was a question she could answer. "It is a bit chaotic, isn't it?" she said. "I believe the evening starts in the auditorium, just over that way." She pointed a well-manicured hand in the proper direction.

"Thanks," said the man. The pair started toward the open doors, then the woman turned back to Cleo. "Are you headed there also?"

"In a moment," replied Cleo. Becoming best buddies with a set of parents was not on her agenda for tonight. Besides, getting into a long conversation could be risky.

She continued her deliberate pace through the halls,

moving between clusters of adults so she wouldn't be noticed walking back and forth, and steering clear of all volunteer student guides. She certainly couldn't afford to run into a classmate tonight. After trying a few different routes, Cleo found a path to Mrs. McMillan's office that was miraculously free of both kids and adults. Satisfied, she went to the auditorium and took a seat near the back.

At precisely 7:30 Mrs. McMillan and two other headmasters stepped onto the stage. Mr. Allen, the short, balding headmaster from the lower school, took the podium first. As the lights lowered to half in the auditorium, the buzzing of the talking parents died down and all eyes went to the speaker. No one noticed the solitary woman in blue quietly exit the room.

Without hesitation, Cleo followed her chosen route to Mrs. McMillan's office, successfully avoiding latecomers and wandering student guides. In front of the office, she took a deep breath and wrapped her fingers around the doorknob. It turned easily and the door opened.

Undercover Cleo took a quick look behind her before stepping into the office and closing the door after her.

Chapter 17

I made it, thought Cleo, taking off her dark glasses and putting them in her handbag. Her time was limited and she walked quickly through Ms. Appleby's outer office into Mrs. McMillan's inner sanctum.

According to Robbi, the ballot box would be locked away in Mrs. McMillan's closet. On Cleo's left she saw two closets, but only one that had a lock. That had to be where the ballot box would be kept.

Now where in the world can I put the camera? wondered Cleo. It would have to be set where the lens would not only see Charles removing the sealed box from the closet, but would also record him switching ballots. Cleo surveyed the room and decided the only logical place to switch ballots would be on top of Mrs. McMillan's desk.

She turned and looked at the wall on her right. A

long, low metal filing cabinet sat on the floor directly opposite the closets. On top of that was a large potted plant that looked very promising.

Cleo knelt in front of the cabinet and winced as her knees protested with a loud pop. It seemed like some part of her body was always clicking or aching these days. Growing pains, her mother had said. Not exactly something Cleo wanted to hear.

She rubbed her knee, then set herself at a height where her eyes were level with the plant. Forming a rectangle with her hands and thumbs like a movie director, she aimed an imaginary camera.

Perfect! Cleo could see the desktop and beyond that the locked closet. She poked through the lower part of the plant, then smiled. *These leaves will definitely hide a camcorder,* she thought.

Cleo allowed herself a moment to gloat. Everything was going perfectly. Now all she had to do was find some hiding places for herself and her friends.

She stood up to the sound of another knee pop, then walked across the room to try the other closet. With luck, and it sure seemed to be on her side tonight, the closet would be empty and large enough to hold several witnesses.

Cleo was reaching for the handle when she heard someone moving in the outer office. She dropped her hand, spun around—and found herself facing Mrs. Mc-Millan who was walking through the doorway.

"Well," said the woman, clearing her throat in surprise, "may I help you?"

Shaking off a moment's fluster, Undercover Cleo

tossed her head, took three steps to Mrs. McMillan's desk, then sat gracefully in one of the seats in front. She crossed her legs and let forth a short sigh of exasperation before speaking. "Well, I certainly hope so," Cleo said haughtily. She spoke in the clipped tones and abrupt manner of Mrs. Evans, the Olivers' snobby upstairs neighbor. "Muffy Bannister." She extended her hand and waited for Mrs. McMillan's shock to wear off enough to take the offered hand and shake.

"You have a child you wish to enroll here at Walton?" the headmistress asked. Mrs. McMillan couldn't help but be suspicious of this woman. It had looked for all the world like Ms. Bannister was trying to snoop in her closet.

"It's a possibility," said "Ms. Bannister." "My daughter Angelica. She'll be four in May, but my husband and I are considering schools now. She's very special and no less than the best education will do."

"I see," said Mrs. McMillan. "I'm the headmistress for the middle school, so you'll probably want to speak to Mr. Allen who heads the lower school, but I can answer most of your questions." The woman smiled with pride. "I'm sure you'll find that Walton has some of the finest teachers in the tri-state area and as a result, our students are first class."

"So I understand," said Undercover Cleo. "You must know, I've already had your school thoroughly researched. What I want to find out from you, is how my daughter will be treated here. Angelica is an extremely delicate child so I'll need assurances that she won't be overworked. Believe me, *my little girl* won't need to do much studying at all. Angelica's so *exceptionally* bright that"—Cleo paused and sat up a little higher in her chair—"there is no doubt in my mind she'll be a straight-A student with very little effort."

Mrs. McMillan was speechless at the audacity of this woman, suggesting that her daughter was so brilliant she wouldn't need to do homework. "Ms. Bannister, our teachers do not assign unreasonable amounts of after-school lessons. However, we do try to prepare our students for what they will face in high school and college and I shouldn't have to tell you that it's a dog-eat-dog world out there."

"Yes, I understand, but you don't know Angelica yet," replied "Ms. Bannister." Cleo asked other questions about school policies that soon had Mrs. McMillan more than a little on the defensive. Meanwhile, Cleo was dying to leave, because she knew she wouldn't be able to keep up the charade much longer.

"Well, thank you for your time, Mrs. . . . so sorry?" Undercover Cleo asked.

"McMillan," answered the headmistress. "Evelyn McMillan. I hope I've answered your questions."

"For now, yes. Obviously, Willard and I have many more schools to visit, but we'll be letting you know our decision as soon as we can."

"If I can help you with anything else . . ." Fortunately for Cleo, Mrs. McMillan was also anxious to end the meeting, though the woman would never allow herself to be ungracious. "I hope we'll have the . . . pleasure of meeting Angelica very soon."

In response, Cleo stood to leave and turned up the

corners of her mouth, imitating that vague false smile people use when they're not happy but are trying to be polite. Just then the headmistress noticed the silver locket around Cleo's neck. In spite of her dislike for "Ms. Bannister," Mrs. McMillan couldn't help remarking, "What a beautiful and unusual piece."

Cleo looked down where the woman's eyes were directed. "Oh, this," said "Ms. Bannister," her right hand flying to the locket. She raised it up to look at it. "It's a family heirloom, passed down for generations. Someday, it will be little Angelica's." She rubbed her thumb and forefinger against the silver oval, trying to squeeze a little more good luck out of it—in a few seconds she'd be out of the office and safe. Undercover Cleo gave Mrs. McMillan a condescending nod, then turned and walked out the door.

Cleo relaxed her rigidly held neck and shoulder muscles and hurried down the hallway in the direction of the front gates. A moment after she had turned a corner, a hand reached out and grabbed her arm.

Whirling around she found Liz Cameron attached to her elbow like a suckerfish. Cleo was sure her nightmare was about to come true, but before she could yank her arm away, Liz started talking.

"Hi, my name's Liz," she said, pointing to her name tag. "I'm one of the student guides tonight. Can I help you?" She showed no sign of recognizing Cleo, but her eyes were filled with a stubborn determination to help this "parent" find her way around school.

"Oh, no, I'm just fine," answered Cleo, trying to make a quick getaway.

But Liz wouldn't hear of it. "No, really. It's a big school so everyone gets lost here at first. Just tell me where you're going next."

Cleo realized the only way to get rid of Liz was to ask for help. "Well, actually, dear, you could point me in the direction of the ladies' room. I'd love to powder my nose."

Liz was delighted. "Just go down the hall and turn left. It's the first, no, the second door on your right after that. The light on this floor isn't the best for putting on lipstick, though, not anywhere as good as the fourth floor. Not that you need any, I mean, you look great," she burbled on. "Oops, 'scuse me, there's another lost parent, I'd better go help. If you need anything else just ask for Liz, okay?"

Cleo thanked the girl and headed toward the bathroom. At the end of the hall, she glanced back to see Liz gesturing to another set of parents. *She's going to be annoying no matter what age she is,* thought Cleo. And with that, "Ms. Bannister" turned away from the bathrooms and went out the side exit to the street.

Cleo was rather proud of herself. She'd accomplished her mission and despite a few sticky situations, no one had recognized her. She couldn't wait to get home so she could continue her research on this "undercover" project.

ALL GUESTS MUST BE ANNOUNCED read the sign in Cleo's lobby. Unless a person lived in the building or was a regular visitor like Robbi, they weren't allowed up to a resident's front door without being announced by the doorman on duty. Cleo had forgotten all about this New York security measure and now she realized that even though she had left the apartment earlier as "Ms. Bannister," she couldn't get back in without being questioned, which might lead to her dad getting called down.

Cleo slowed as she approached the front entrance in hopes that she might luck out. She knew there were times when a person could sneak in, like when the doorman was preoccupied with people arriving or leaving in a taxi. Cleo also knew she would have to time her move perfectly so she settled into a bench across the street to watch and wait.

Fifteen minutes later she was getting worried. No one had gone in or out of the apartment and her bus stop bench wasn't comfortable at all. How much longer was she going to have to wait until the doorman was distracted? Ten minutes? An hour? A day?

Undercover Cleo stood and smoothed out her silk skirt. She had to find another way into the building.

What could be sillier, she wondered, *than sneaking into my own home?*

Cleo crossed the street and walked slowly past the front entrance along the length of the building. Terry was at his desk, right where he was supposed to be. Then as she passed a few steps beyond the north edge of her building she realized she had another option. The service entrance.

Old apartment buildings usually had a separate entrance and elevator for deliveries—groceries, oversize packages, even furniture. If Cleo could get through the gate into the back courtyard, she might be able to take the service elevator up to her apartment without being seen.

She pushed hard on the entrance gate. Locked. Cleo peered through the vertical bars into the cement "backyard." Maybe there was a way the lock could be opened from inside.

She snaked her arm through the bars and it went in up to the elbow, then stuck fast. She switched arms and tried a different slot. This time, her arm popped through the bars up to her shoulder. For once, Cleo was thankful to have long skinny arms.

Her fingers groped for a doorknob, but discovered instead something that felt like a key on a wind-up toy. It was the handle of the lock. With only two of her fingers able to reach the thin knob, she didn't quite have the leverage to turn it. Cleo shoved a little harder, jamming her face against the bars, and just managed to get the position she needed. Her thumb pushed against the underside of the key while her index finger pulled the top. To her relief, she felt a click.

Cleo opened the door an inch, then slid her arm out from between the iron bars. She took a quick look around, stepped through the gate, and walked the four steps to the entrance at the basement level. Cleo knew this door was left propped open for ventilation until nine o'clock when the laundry room was closed for the night. She pressed her ear to the crack of the door and heard nothing but the sound of the dryers in the laundry room.

Quickly pulling the door open, the girl raced down

the corridor and pushed the call button for the service elevator. The clanking of ancient gears as the machinery started up was not a comforting sound and usually brought to mind images of a tired old machine that was about to fall into pieces. But right now, the horrible creaking was music to Cleo's ears—it meant she was almost home free.

After riding up to her floor, Cleo took her keys from her mother's handbag and quietly unlocked the back door. Nortrud would have gone home right after the dinner dishes were done and the teenager knew she could pretty much count on her father's total concentration on work.

She was right. She could hear her father working in his office and it sounded like the rest of the apartment was empty. She slipped off her shoes and crept toward her bedroom.

Cleo got as far as the kitchen before she was noticed. Phoebe, who had been dead asleep underneath the table, jerked awake, her ears perking straight up in the air.

Thump! Thump! Seeing "Ms. Bannister" sneaking into her house, Phoebe sent out the universal rabbit warning signal that she produced by stomping her large back feet. Cleo bit down on her bottom lip to keep from giggling as she went toward her frightened pet.

"Phoebe, it's me," she whispered. "Come here."

Cleo leaned forward to pick up the beast who became even more alarmed as the "stranger" approached. The animal dashed down the hall and into the TV room. Cleo followed in hopes of calming the terrified rabbit, but there was no appeasing the beast. She sat under Mr. Oliver's easy chair thumping madly.

"Hey, Bun, what's wrong?" called Mr. Oliver from his office. "Should I come out and look for a burglar in the house?"

He laughed at his own joke, but to Cleo's horror, the next sound she heard was the squeaking of her dad's chair as he stood up. Every muscle in Cleo's body tensed and she launched herself back toward the kitchen, praying her father wasn't actually going to investigate.

"Where are you, Phoebe?" called her father. Cleo heard Mr. Oliver's voice in the hall, just as she made it back to the kitchen where she hid behind the door. A moment later the wall phone jangled right beside her head, startling Cleo so much she inadvertently jerked her knee, banging the door between the kitchen and the dining room.

She watched in horror as the door swung back and forth, creaking loudly.

Chapter 18

Cleo wasn't sure if what she heard next was her heart pounding or her father's footsteps as he hurried back into his office to answer his phone.

"Cleo! Is that you in the kitchen?" Mr. Oliver bellowed.

Cleo had no choice but to answer. "Yeah, Dad."

"Robbi's on the phone."

"Okay," called Cleo. She picked up the phone, thinking, *Please, Dad, stay in your office now.* "Hey, Rob."

"So? What happened?" asked Robbi. "Did you get into Mrs. McMillan's office? I want all the gory details."

"Listen, I'll tell you everything, but I gotta call you back." Cleo spoke softly. She hung up and hurried to the sanctuary of her room.

Safely inside, she sat down to catch her breath. A split second later she heard her father's voice again. Mr. Oliver called out, "Cleo? Where are you? In your room?"

"Yeah." Moving as fast as she could, Cleo threw the scarf, wig, and shoes into her open closet. Her father's voice came closer as he spoke until he was right outside her door.

"Cleo, did I see you wearing . . . ? Come out here for a minute, would you?" asked her father.

"Just a sec, Dad," Cleo said, dipping her fingers into cold cream and globbing it on her face. She yanked several tissues from a box on her bedside table and wiped her face. She started to unbutton the suit jacket, when her father knocked again.

"Cleo?" This time there was more urgency in his voice.

Reluctantly she rebuttoned the jacket and opened her door. "Hi," Cleo said, hanging her head sheepishly.

"I was right. You *were* wearing your mother's suit."

Cleo opened her mouth to explain, but her father continued before she had a chance. "She was wearing that very same dress the first time I saw her. In fact, she made it herself, did you know that?"

Cleo looked down at the suit. That explained why there was no label. Her mind was working full tilt to come up with some explanation for being dressed up, but she didn't have to worry. Mr. Oliver was back in the past.

"Your mother was sixteen and had come to spend the summer in New York with her Aunt Kathleen. Hard to believe that crazy woman used to run a travel agency, isn't it? Anyway, after a week of shopping and museum hopping, you can imagine, your mother was bored to death, so she started going to the office with her aunt to help out. And one of the clients of the travel agency, during your mother's brief tenure there, just happened to be yours truly—the dashing, the brilliant, the charismatic Scott Oliver.''

Cleo laughed. She knew the story of how her parents had met, but she never tired of hearing it.

Mr. Oliver had been a student at Columbia's School of Journalism and had gone to pick up his ticket home for the summer holiday. Though it had been strictly a business encounter, neither of Cleo's parents had forgotten it and when they met at a party two years later—Alexa, by then a well-known model, and Scott, a junior reporter at a small metropolitan newspaper—they knew they were meant to be together.

Mr. Oliver sighed and looked closely at his daughter. "You look just as beautiful in this suit as your mother did. I didn't know she still kept it around." He tousled Cleo's hair, then turned and walked back to his office, lost in a cloud of memories.

Mom wore this suit when she was just a teenager? No wonder it fits so well, Cleo thought. *But that means when Mom was a kid, she must have been shaped just like me.* Cleo wondered if this meant that someday she would look as great as her mother did now.

She started picking up her room, wondering what Robbi would say when she told her about the suit. Robbi! She had forgotten to call her best friend. Cleo decided her room could wait and she sat down with the phone.

"Rob, you'll never believe what happened tonight." Cleo launched into her encounters with Mrs. McMillan and Liz during Open House. "I thought I would be really scared and, Rob, you'll probably think I'm a total case, but I actually had fun. And you know what? I think I was pretty good." Cleo was usually too insecure to praise herself, but tonight she felt especially proud of what she had done. "Oh and guess what? I found a place to hide the camera."

"Wow. So we're definitely doing this tomorrow night?" asked her friend.

"Absolutely," said Cleo. "Listen, I should call Jason and let him know. See you in the morning, okay?"

Cleo went to the kitchen to get the phone book where her mother kept the Walton eighth-grade phone list that had every parent's name, address, and phone number. She dialed Jason's number.

Hearing the ring on the other end of the line made Cleo suddenly nervous and without thinking, she hung up, instantly regretting her action. *Great,* she thought, *I can't call now, or Jason will know it was me who hung up.* Disgusted, she ambled to the family room to wait a suitable amount of time before dialing again.

She flopped onto the couch, picked up the remote controller, and absentmindedly surfed through the channels. Settling on a reality-based cop show, she watched three burly policemen batter down a door in pursuit of a suspected bank robber. Then she realized there was yet another hitch in her plan. How were they going to get into Mrs. McMillan's office tomorrow night? Staying and hiding in the school until after hours was one thing, but wouldn't all the rooms be locked up for the night? *Oh, why is everything turning out to be so complicated?* she wondered.

Too agitated to concentrate on the television program, Cleo stood and pulled a photo album off a shelf over the entertainment system. It was her favorite book, one filled with some of her mother's "outtake" shots and funnier print layouts. Alexa had a healthy sense of humor about her job and saved a whole book of "blooper" pictures. The nice photos had all been kept and filed away by Cleo's grandmother who had a spare room full of scrapbooks in her Florida condo.

It's too bad we can't just ask someone to open the door for us, thought Cleo. She flipped through the pages, smiling at one shot of her mother, taken at the exact moment when her eyes were half open and her smile incomplete. *I guess the spare keys are out of the question now,* Cleo thought to herself.

Just then, her eyes rested on a magazine layout for sleepwear in which Alexa was dressed as various storybook characters such as Goldilocks and Sleeping Beauty. On the next page her mother was decked out as Cinderella. Cleo stared at the picture for a moment, then laughed out loud. She had her solution. Confidently she put the album back in its place and dialed Jason's number.

Chapter 19

Eager to vote as soon as possible, Cleo rushed to school on Tuesday morning and arrived twenty minutes early. Voting booths were set up in the gymnasium on the sixth floor where they would stay open all day so that students could vote whenever they had a chance. The kids lined up and when it was their turn, they gave their names to one of a pair of students from the upper school who were acting as election officials. The voter would then be handed a ballot and have his or her name checked off a list.

Cleo watched the white curtains of the polling booths flutter back and forth as students entered and exited and she realized it hadn't been necessary to rush. The line quickly and in no time at all she was giving her the upper school officials.

liver, eighth grade.''

The high school girl ran her pen down the printout of the eighth-graders' names. "Cleopatra Oliver?" she said and looked up at Cleo. "Your name is really Cleopatra?"

Cleo rolled her eyes. "Yes." People always said her name like it was weird, but she liked it anyway. Her parents had rented the movie *Cleopatra* with Elizabeth Taylor and Richard Burton the day before their daughter was born. When the Oliver baby popped out with a full head of dark hair and dramatically white skin, there was no question in either Scott's or Alexa's mind what their little girl's name should be.

The high school girl handed Cleo a ballot and a pencil. "Bring back the pencil when you're done, okay?"

Cleo looked at the white square of paper printed with the names of the candidates, then stepped up to the booth. She pulled the thin white curtain shut, making sure there were no cracks in it. *Not that it matters much,* she supposed, but it was the principle of the thing.

She checked off the names of students she wanted for the offices of representative, treasurer, secretary, and vice president. Cleo rearranged the pencil in her hand before marking her choice for president. Then she made a bold "X" in the box next to Jason's name. Afraid it wasn't enough, she blackened the entire square, then circled it for emphasis. Now, even erasing wouldn't take the mark off the paper.

Satisfied, she folded the paper in half, then in half again, whisked back the curtain, walked out of the booth, and handed the pencil back to the election official. "Thank you, Cleopatra." The older girl smiled at Cleo. "Hey, it's a really cool name."

Cleo's mouth dropped open in surprise before she managed to say, "Thanks." She hadn't been prepared for a compliment, but what a welcome change. *Maybe it's a good omen,* she thought as she dropped her ballot into the ballot box, then poked it securely in. Feeling like she'd done her civic duty, Cleo headed down to her locker to pick up her books for first period.

Everyone in the halls was talking about the election. From the number of comments she heard, it sounded to Cleo like the votes were evenly divided between Jason and Charles. She wondered if it would make a difference in Charles's plans for the evening if he thought he was ahead. *Maybe he'll be so confident he'll call off his ballot box theft,* thought Cleo. *Nah, he's too desperate.*

Someone gave her a rib-tickling pinch from behind. "Did you vote yet?" asked Robbi as she came around in front of her friend.

"Yeah," replied Cleo. "You?"

"Not yet. I'm on my way right now. Who'd you vote for?"

"That's privileged information," Cleo teased. "I'll see you in math, okay?" She was about to leave when she saw a very curious sight.

Charles was coming up the stairs, and not only was he without his cronies, Andy and Michael, but he was chatting very buddy-buddy like with Jason Garrett. The leader of the Three Stooges was even patting Jason on the back as the boys headed toward the gym. Jason seemed slightly suspicious of his rival, but smiled and nodded as they walked together.

"Hello-o-o. What's wrong with this picture?" whispered Robbi.

"I don't get it," said Cleo. She eyed the boys as they came toward her.

"Hello." Jason waved to the girls as he approached.

"Hi, Jason," said Cleo. "I thought you said you were going to the dentist today?"

"I am, after first period. I decided to stop by so I could vote first. Just in case."

"Hi, Cleo. Good to see you," said Charles, not quite looking up enough to make eye contact. "Hey, Robbi."

"Hey, Charles," Robbi said, not bothering to hide the suspicion in her voice. After the boys had walked past she said quietly in Cleo's ear, "Now I know something's up. Has Charles Maxwell ever once said 'hi' to you?"

Cleo shook her head. Robbi was right, something was very wrong here. Charles Maxwell was only nice when he wanted something.

Jason turned back to the girls. "Have you two cast your votes already?"

Cleo nodded and Robbi was quick to reply, "No, but I think I'll wait until later. The line's kind of long right now."

"Okay. Until later then," said Jason.

"Ditto," said Charles as he stepped in front of Jason in the line.

Cleo and Robbi stood watching for a moment, trying

to figure out what they had missed.

"This smells," said Cleo.

"Worse than yesterday's diapers," agreed Robbi. "What should we do?"

"What can we do?" said Cleo. "Tell Mrs. McMillan that Charles is being too nice? I don't think so. But he's definitely got something up his sleeve. Come on, let's get to class." She turned to go, but Robbi remained stationary.

"You go on ahead," said Robbi. "I think I'll try to vote now. The line doesn't look so long after all." She smiled and waved her friend along.

"What are you going to do?" asked Cleo. She knew her friend too well to believe Robbi had simply changed her mind.

"Nothing," proclaimed Robbi. "Just go." She gave her friend a gentle push toward the stairs. Cleo took one last look and noticed that as Robbi stepped into line, she positioned herself behind several taller students so that neither Charles nor Jason could see her, but the girl was still close enough to watch everything the two boys did. *That's Robbi,* thought Cleo, *always using her height, or lack of it, to her advantage.*

The small girl kept a sharp eye on the two candidates. Something was fishy and she was determined to find out what it was. She had to know why Charles was being so nice to the very person he planned to cheat later that night.

As the line moved forward, she glanced at her watch, hoping she wouldn't have to abandon her mission to get to class. Robbi peeked around the girl in front of her to see Charles had just reached the head of the line. After receiving his ballot, he turned back to Jason and asked, ''Would you mind watching my bag while I go in?'' He gestured to the black leather backpack on the floor at his feet.

Jason shrugged. ''No problem.''

When Charles emerged from the booth, he stuffed his ballot in the box, then walked to Jason. ''Thanks,'' he said, ''I'll watch yours for you.'' He tugged lightly at Jason's pack that hung over the boy's right shoulder.

''Oh, okay. Thanks,'' said Jason who let the pack slide into Charles's hand before entering the booth. Robbi watched as Charles, carrying both his own bag and Jason's, moved casually away to the side of the gym to wait.

This is not Charles Maxwell, Robbi thought. *What is going on?* For the life of her, she couldn't figure out what he was up to.

Someone tapped her on the shoulder, and she whirled around slightly startled. ''Keep the line moving,'' said the boy behind her.

Robbi quickly went forward three steps, closing the gap between her and the girl ahead of her. She turned back to check on Charles—just in time to see him pulling the drawstring on Jason's bag. *Why is he closing Jason's bag,* Robbi wondered. *Maybe he took something?!*

Robbi pulled back into line, safely hidden between other students as her brain went into action. What had she really seen? Could Charles have stolen something? *But no,* when she thought about it, *Charles wasn't hold-*

ing anything in his hand. He must have put something in!

Robbi's brain raced with possibilities of what Charles might have stuck in Jason's pack. *A bomb! No, too silly. The spare keys? No, Charles still needs the keys to get into school and Mrs. McMillan's office.*

The teenager could not come up with a reason for Charles to have been messing with Jason's backpack and the more she thought about it, the more uncertain she became that she had even witnessed him doing that. If only the guy behind her hadn't distracted her. She turned to give the boy a nasty look when Jason came out of the booth and Robbi ducked behind the group in front of her. No sense drawing Jason's attention now.

Maybe, when Charles put the bag down on the floor something fell out and he was just putting it back in. Robbi's own book bag seemed to weigh as much as she did and she knew anyone would have a problem carrying two of them. She was still trying to guess what Charles had been doing when she discovered it was her turn to vote. She took her ballot into the booth and marked her votes in record time, but when she came out the two boys had left.

After dropping her ballot in the box, Robbi rushed away to class and by the time the bell rang, she had forgotten all about the strange incident.

The commotion began right after first period. There was a strange buzz in the air and it didn't seem to be solely about the election. Cleo and Robbi went to their respective lockers, then met up outside of English class.

"What's going on?" Cleo asked. "We must be missing out on something . . . again." She hadn't forgotten about seeing Jason and Charles together.

"Definitely," replied Robbi. The two girls pressed into a group of kids gathered around a freckle-faced boy who seemed to be the center of information. "Hey, Mark, what's the deal?" Robbi asked. The boy was in her social studies class.

"I can't believe you haven't heard," he told them. "Someone got into Mr. Fleming's office and stole the science test out of his briefcase. Rumor has it, it was Jason Garrett. Someone left an anonymous note under the door saying they'd seen Garrett leave the office with papers in his hand and he put them in his book bag." The boy was very pleased with himself for being the messenger of such shocking news.

"Mrs. McMillan is out looking for Garrett right now," he said, about to head off when Cleo grabbed his elbow and held tight.

"I don't believe that," she said. "Where'd you hear all this?"

"Whoa, chill, okay?" said Mark. He pulled his arm away and rubbed his elbow. "I was standing in McMillan's office when Fleming came in and told her about the missing test and showed her the note. It's true." He shrugged and moved quickly down the hall to catch up with his friends.

"Oh, my gosh," said Robbi. "Now I get it."

Chattering at the speed of light she told Cleo what she had seen in the gym. "Charles must have been putting the stolen test in Jason's pack."

"And I'll bet you he's behind the note blaming Jason, too," said Cleo, who was now pacing in the empty hall.

"What a total loser," said Robbi. "Maxwell must be so desperate that switching the ballots isn't enough. He had to come up with a backup plan." She shook her head.

"He must have used the spare set of keys to get in and steal the test." Then Cleo stopped in midstride. "Oh, no, what if Mrs. McMillan finds the test in Jason's bag?"

"He'll be automatically disqualified from the election," said Robbi, "and that would be the least of his problems."

Cleo turned to Robbi. "Jason's at the dentist, remember? We've got to get to him before he gets back or he'll be in real trouble."

"That's for sure," said Robbi. "Maybe we should wait at the front gates for him?"

"No," said Cleo, "that could be too late. I'll try to call him. He said his dentist's name was Dr. Chiu, right? We'd better warn him."

The girls hurried to the pay phone at the end of the hall. Cleo dialed 411 and asked the operator for the number of a Dr. C-h-i-u. When the recorded message with the phone number came on, Cleo whispered to Robbi, "Five-five-five two-six-five-four. Got it?"

Robbi repeated the number and nodded her head. Cleo dropped a quarter in the slot. "Okay now, what was that number?" she asked.

Robbi told her and watched to make sure her friend pushed the right buttons.

"It's ringing," Cleo whispered. "Hello, I'm trying to find Jason Garrett. He's supposed to have an appointment this morning. Thanks." She put her hand over the receiver and spoke to her friend. "They're paging him." Then she cocked her head back to the listening position. "What? Not there yet? Uh, no, there's no message." She hung up slowly.

"So what now?" asked Robbi.

"I guess I should hang around and try to call again in a few minutes," answered Cleo.

"Well, okay, but I've got to get to English." The focus of class right now was one of Robbi's favorite subjects—debating. She had worked very hard on this particular assignment and today she'd have her chance to get up in front of her classmates and present her well-researched arguments. There was no way Robbi would miss class today, not even for an adventure.

Cleo nodded understandingly. "Okay. You go on." She picked up the phone to dial again. This time the line was busy.

The next time Cleo called, a different voice answered, curt and short-tempered. "University Dental Center."

"I'd like to speak to a patient, Jason Garrett."

There was a pause and Cleo could hear papers rustling before the voice spoke again. "I'm sorry, he's with the doctor having a filling put in."

"But this is really important."

"I'm sorry the patient cannot be disturbed," the voice said with finality.

Cleo hung up, realizing, *I've got no choice. I've got to warn Jason in person.*

She was familiar with the area around Columbia Presbyterian Medical Center because the Olivers' family doctor was there. The address—169th Street and Broadway—was a little forbidding but Cleo had been there many times with her parents. She knew she could ride the subway to a stop directly in front of the Med Center and if she caught an express train, she might even be there and back before lunch.

Cleo ran to her locker and emptied her backpack. She needed to travel fast and light and that just wasn't possible lugging French, math, social studies, English, and science books. She slammed her locker shut and ran down the stairs to the first floor.

At the front door she checked around for Mr. Horner, the school security guard, but he was nowhere to be seen. He patrolled the courtyard during lunch hours and breaks, anytime students were around, but his job was more to keep strangers out than to keep students in.

Tiptoeing down the hall, Cleo spotted the guard in Mrs. McMillan's outer office, sipping coffee and joking with Ms. Appleby. The coast was clear.

Cleo dashed through the Walton gates onto West End Avenue.

Chapter 20

She didn't slow down until she reached the subway station on 72nd Street and Broadway. After pulling out a school pass that allowed her to ride the subway during school hours, she flashed it at the transit worker in the token booth and was buzzed through a turnstile.

New York was in the middle of an Indian summer and the air down on the platform was hot and smelly. Cleo felt her skin get sticky as she waited, and she hoped the train would come soon so she could get into an air-conditioned car. She knew it shouldn't be long—the subway ran every few minutes during the day—but even so, she walked back and forth and leaned out over the tracks to see if a train was on the way. Seeing nothing but the black tunnel, she resumed pacing.

Am I nuts? she wondered. *Cutting school because there* might *be a stolen test in Jason's bag?* Cleo started back toward the turnstile to leave the subway station. *Maybe I should just go back to Walton and wait.* Jason's bag might be empty and this would end up being a wasted trip, not to mention the fact that she'd have to think up some excuse for missing classes.

On the other hand, and the thought obsessed her, the stolen test could very well be in Jason's bag and no matter how innocent he was, it would be hard to prove otherwise. Cleo knew she couldn't let Jason take that chance, because by the time his name was cleared, it would be too late and he would be sure to lose the election.

She turned back to the train tracks, her decision made. She would first find out if the papers were in Jason's bag and, if they were, she was going to get them out before they got him into trouble he didn't deserve.

The roar of the subway train and the squeal of rusty brakes jolted Cleo back to earth. She stepped into the train and grabbed one of the metal ''straps'' to steady herself for the ride. In a few minutes she'd be at her destination.

By the time she reached the subway stop at 168th Street, Cleo had decided she couldn't go into the dental office as herself. She didn't have an appointment so someone would be sure to question her about why she wasn't in school and she'd almost certainly get into some kind of trouble. She knew she needed to get past the receptionists and dentists, but she had an idea how to do it.

When the door to the subway train closed behind Cleo, she was on her way to another ''covert operation.'' After the success of ''Operation Open House'' last night, she had enough confidence to try this on the spur of the moment.

Cleo walked directly to a small store across the street from the Med Center. She had seen the place several times before on trips with her parents and now, as she always did, she paused to look at the display window.

Cleo loved walking down Fifth Avenue and staring into the legendary windows of Tiffany's, FAO Schwartz, or Lord & Taylor at Christmastime, but none of them came close to this weird display. The surgical supply house window was one of the most bizarre Cleo had ever seen.

The contents of the display hadn't changed for as long as the girl could remember. There was dust on everything and the boxes of gauze and cotton balls had all turned yellow from years of sunlight. There were large and small bandages, canes and walkers, tweezers, forceps, and scissors of all sizes and shapes. When Cleo had been younger, one of her favorite things had been the little round mirrors set on the end of a chrome handle that dentist, use to examine teeth. Some hardworking employee of this mom-and-pop store had taken the time to arrange a peculiar display of these tools, setting them side by side in a sunflowerlike pattern with their handles poking outward. The hundreds of tiny mirrors caught the sun's rays and flashed them back at the passersby on the street.

But there wasn't much time to admire the window "sculpture" today and Cleo hurried inside to the counter and asked for several items. Her disguise would be fairly simple, and a few minutes later she left the store and went to the emergency entrance of the hospital. As she expected, the place was bustling. No one paid any attention to the girl as she slipped past the harried reception nurses, down a hallway, and into an empty rest room where she unwrapped her purchases and quickly put them on.

Two minutes later, decked out in a medical cap and blue gown, a surgeon's mask dangling around her neck, Cleo was a close likeness to the dozens of Columbia dental students who worked in the clinic as part of their training. The teenager looked down and smiled when she saw her jeans sticking out underneath the gown. It only added to the authenticity of her disguise. Cleo's final touch was a pair of thick-lensed glasses that she wore low on her nose. The lenses made it a little hard to see, but they markedly altered her appearance. Between the glasses on her face, the mask dangling under her chin, and the cap covering her hair, she felt like she could have fooled her grandmother.

Cleo backtracked to the emergency-room waiting area, then walked through it into a maze of hallways. She needed to find the front entrance of the hospital. Holding as straight a course as possible, she made it to the familiar front reception area and the row of elevators nearby. Checking the directory, Cleo saw that the dental clinic was on the seventh and eighth floors.

Stepping into the elevator, she pushed ''7'' and went up. *So now that I'm in, what do I do?* she wondered.

The reception desk was directly in front of her when the elevator doors opened. Off to her left, she saw a clump of four dentists talking and walking quickly toward a large pair of double doors. A sign over the doors read, ORAL SURGERY—AUTHORIZED PERSONNEL ONLY. Cleo saw her chance and fell into step just a little behind the foursome.

Moving with them through the wide doors she suddenly panicked. A guard sat at a desk ahead of them and he was checking IDs.

Cleo ducked her head, about to turn and run back to the elevators when she had an idea. As she neared the guard, she slipped her hand in her jeans pocket, wrapping it around her plastic-coated school subway ID. Making the move as casual and practiced as she could, Cleo briefly flashed the card at the man, half hiding it with her hand. At the same time, she gave him a broad friendly smile.

He smiled back and Cleo was in.

A moment later the tall girl found herself in the midst of chaos. No one moved slowly here; there was far too much to be done. Cleo picked up her own pace moving rapidly down the corridor. *Now, how am I ever going to find Jason in this place?*

A double door in front of Cleo burst open and two people in hospital blues came straight toward her. "I never thought there was so much involved in third molar extraction," said a short-haired female student.

The other dental intern, a young man, nodded wearily, then lifted his chin in Cleo's direction. "Hey, if you're the relief, there's an emergency coming in—a kid got his upper incisors broken in a fight. Good luck, it's going to be a tough one."

Undercover Cleo knew she had to look like she was in total shock, but managed to come up with a reply. "I hope it's not too bad. This is my first day." *And, boy, is that ever the truth,* she thought.

The two students raised their eyebrows and their smiles were visible even through the masks. "Don't worry," said the girl, "you'll do fine. Morris is your resident and he's great. He should be here any minute. Oh, you can drop your backpack in the locker room." Cleo followed the students into the small room.

"Thanks," said Undercover Cleo. As she hung her pack on a hook on the wall, she thought, *I've got to get out of here before someone drags me in to do a root canal.* The ambiance of a dental office was creepy enough, but a place where they performed oral surgery—forget it. She shook off the thought as she exited the locker room.

Not knowing where to begin, Cleo chose the first door she saw and cautiously peeked in.

A large woman sat in the chair, head back and mouth open. The dentist had what looked like all ten of his fingers in her mouth. "So, Shirley, how are the kids?" he asked her.

Cleo giggled as she hurried away down the hall. *Why do dentists always start a conversation when it's impossible to answer?* she wondered.

She checked two more rooms before finding the right one. Jason was seated facing away from the door, mouth open, with a very intense-looking dentist poised over him. Cleo sucked in her breath when she spotted Jason's brown pack on the floor, lying against the wall just inside the door.

What should I do? she wondered. *This isn't exactly the time or the place to give Jason another farfetched story.* Besides blowing her disguise, it wouldn't be too swift getting caught sneaking into the clinic. She didn't want anyone, except her best friend, to know she was going around undercover.

Cleo realized that if she could get the papers without Jason ever knowing anything about them, there would be no question of his innocence when Mrs. McMillan caught up with him back at school. Undercover Cleo crossed her fingers for luck and barged in the room. "Dr. Morris?" she asked, knowing from the two interns she'd run into earlier that Dr. Morris would be elsewhere.

"No," said the dentist, looking up from his work, "He's usually in surgery A or B, but I'm not even sure he's in yet."

"Thanks," said Cleo and as the doctor went back to his work she also turned to go. But before she took a step, she put out her right foot and hooked a toe under a strap of Jason's bag. Then, imitating the soccer players she had seen the week before, the girl lifted her foot and the bag from the floor until it was high enough for her to grab with a free hand. Shielding the bag with her body, she walked briskly out the door toward the locker room, which, to her great relief, was empty.

Her fingers shaking, she loosened the leather drawstrings. "Come on, come on," she muttered to herself, tugging at the leather until it gaped open.

It was a curious feeling, snooping into someone else's pack, and Cleo was determined to see only the offending test papers, if they existed. She'd hate to think of someone poking about in her bag, but then, this was a special situation. Cleo saw books and papers all lined up neatly. A flip of white caught her eye, but when she pulled it out, she saw it was a copy of Jason's speech. She was beginning to think that maybe she and Robbi had been wrong about Charles, when she saw another flash of white under the books at the bottom of the backpack.

A dozen pages had been folded in half lengthwise and Cleo gingerly opened them and peeked at the heading of a page. WALTON SCIENCE ACHIEVEMENT TEST—GRADE 8. She hurriedly refolded the stolen test and shoved it into her own backpack. *Great. Now watch* me *get caught with this,* she thought as she pulled the drawstring tight on Jason's bag.

Okay, I only have to put this back in the room with Jason and I'm out of here. Undercover Cleo went to the door, when someone on the other side opened it, almost hitting her in the face.

"Oh, dreadfully sorry," apologized Jason. "You all right?" He looked up at her with concern.

"Fine, yeah," said Undercover Cleo, slipping into a heavy Brooklyn accent. She couldn't stop herself from smiling and was half hoping that Jason would recognize her underneath the surgical garb.

But his mind was elsewhere and all he said was, "I'm looking for my pack. I thought I'd taken it in the other room with me, but it's not there."

"This it?" Undercover Cleo picked up Jason's leather pack. "I found it lyin' in the hall and brought it here for safekeepin'. The cleaning guy musta moved it or sumpin'."

"Thanks. I was afraid someone might have taken it," said Jason. Then he laughed. "I suppose no one would really want a bunch of schoolbooks though, would they?"

"Not likely," agreed Cleo, feeling a little disappointed but also thrilled that Jason didn't know who she was.

"Going out?" the boy said, gesturing for her to go on ahead and holding the door open for her. Out in the hall, he said, "Thanks again," and headed off toward the reception desk, leaving the girl looking after him.

Just then a team of nurses and students came careening around a corridor pushing someone on a gurney.

"Out of the way, out of the way," shouted a nurse, and the group scrambled past her and into an operating room. *Must be the emergency they were talking about,* Cleo realized. *Time to make an exit.* Clutching her bag tightly, she started toward the double doors that would take her back to the elevators. She was almost at the exit and past the security guard when the door to the operating room opened and somebody yelled, "Hey, you! Get back over here."

Cleo whirled around. "Me?" she said in a panic.

"No, Santa Claus," retorted the young man.

Cleo tried to explain, "But . . ." But the other student wouldn't hear any excuses.

"Just move it, on the double," he said, waiting in the doorway, watching to make sure Cleo wouldn't disappear.

A friendly looking man dressed in surgical garb came out of the locker room. Seeing Cleo standing in shock, he beckoned to her. He smiled as she approached and said, "I'm Dr. Morris. Here, let me put this away for you." He took Cleo's backpack and quickly set it in the locker room. Then he made the same gesture with his hand that Jason had made, inviting her to enter the operating room.

Chapter 21

Cleo swallowed hard and went through the operating-room doors. "Scrub up and stand over here," said Dr. Morris, motioning to a place beside the operating table.

Half in a daze, Cleo imitated the student who had mentioned Santa Claus as he washed with surgical foam from a dispenser and pulled on a pair of thin latex gloves. Taking the place where she had been directed she stood quietly, holding in her breath as she tried not to watch the proceedings.

Cleo saw that the patient was a ten-year-old boy who had his front teeth broken. Dr. Morris was asking opinions from the students as to whether they thought he should extract the teeth or try to save them. One at a time all three students in the operating room said, "Extract."

When he got to Cleo she couldn't help feeling sorry for the boy. She knew she wouldn't want to lose her two front teeth. Her answer, based only on emotion, was, "Save them."

"Well, at least there's *someone* here with enough common sense to become a dentist," said Dr. Morris, giving Cleo an approving nod. "All right, too many heads around, all nonessential bodies out of the room." Feeling very nonessential indeed, Cleo followed the other students toward the door.

"Oh, miss," said Dr. Morris, "I'd like to have a word with you later on. I'll see you in my office."

Ignoring the comments of "How'd you know?" and "Great going," Cleo retrieved her backpack and walked quickly down the hall. As she approached the pair of double doors, another female student came through them and headed straight toward Cleo with a very confused look on her face. "Do you know where I would find Dr. Morris?" she asked. "I'm supposed to report to him. It's my first day."

Undercover Cleo pointed back to the door she had just come out of and said, "Just wait in his office. He'll speak to you later." With that, Cleo sailed past the guard and out of the restricted area of the clinic.

There was no way she was going to take a chance and wait for the elevator. Instead, Cleo took the stairs, bolting down them three at a time. On the way, she peeled off her disguise and stuffed everything into her backpack.

"Freedom!" she shouted as she burst out of the hospital doors and onto the street. In minutes she was down in the subway on board a southbound train. Now, all she had to do was figure out what to do with the stolen test.

When she emerged at the 72nd Street stop, Cleo automatically glanced up at the digital time and temperature display on top of the Apple Bank on 73rd Street. It was almost noon. Perfect timing. Kids would be swarming out of the classrooms for lunch in ten minutes and Cleo knew she had a good shot at getting back into Walton unnoticed. It was hard to believe she still had to finish out the rest of her classes—so much had happened this morning, it felt like it was time to go home for the day.

She stopped in a small stationery store and bought a large manila envelope. Outside the shop, she put the achievement test in the envelope and sealed it shut. She took a pencil from her bag, and being right-handed, she used her left hand to write in block letters, TO MR. FLEMING. Cleo planned to slip the envelope under the door of the teacher's room.

She timed her return just right, easily blending into the crowds, and went to her locker to exchange her backpack for her lunch bag. Robbi showed up by her side a few moments later.

"Come on," said Cleo, grabbing her friend and pulling her to a secluded corner. "I've got the test," she whispered. "You were right. Charles put it in Jason's bag. Jason doesn't know anything about it and I want to leave it that way, but you've got to help me get this"—and she flashed the manila envelope at her friend—"back into Mr. Fleming's room."

"I was wondering what happened," Robbi said. "Jason just got back and they didn't find anything in his bag. Now they're saying he was framed."

"Good. Then he's off the hook," Cleo said, breathing a sigh of relief. "Come on, I can't really relax until these papers are 'out of my possesion,' as you would say. Everyone's at lunch now, we should be able to slip it under the science-room door." She rolled the envelope up and stuck it in her lunch bag.

The two girls went down to the computer and science rooms on the third floor. There were no lockers in this area and being lunch period, the floor was fairly empty. The girls knew it should stay that way for about the next hour.

They went straight to Mr. Fleming's room. It was impossible to see anything through the frosted glass on the closed door. "Do you think he's in there?" asked Cleo.

"Uh-uh," answered Robbi. "He's got to be at lunch."

Cleo opened her bag and pulled the envelope from inside. She glanced around to be sure there was no one watching.

"Why do I feel so guilty?" she asked her friend.

"I don't know, but can we just do this and get out of here," said Robbi. "You can think about it later." She was clearly nervous. "If we get caught, I won't be able to be on the debating team."

Cleo bent down and put the envelope on the floor. "Ready?" she asked.

Robbi nodded her head and watched as Cleo sent the

slim packet sliding under the door. The girls gave each other a high-five and started for the stairs when they heard Mr. Fleming's voice.

"Who's there? Come on in," the teacher called.

Cleo and Robbi looked at each other in terror. When they heard his footsteps approach the door, they took off, running as fast as their legs would carry them.

Chapter 22

Cleo and Robbi just managed to reach the stairwell when Mr. Fleming's door opened and they ran down the steps all the way to the lunchroom on the first floor. Trying to hide the fact that they were out of breath, they strolled into the cafeteria and took seats in the back.

"That was too close," panted Cleo.

"I'll say," replied Robbi, then her tiny face crinkled up with worry. "Do you think he saw us?"

"I'm sure he didn't," said Cleo. "I didn't hear the door open until we were in the stairs . . . I think." She tried to smile, but her nerves wouldn't let her.

"We'd better eat then," said Robbi. "This could be our last meal as Walton students." She unwrapped her lunch, today only a plain peanut butter and banana sandwich, and took a big bite.

The girls waited apprehensively during lunch, half expecting to be called to the office and grilled about the newly turned-up test papers, but nothing happened. No one seemed to suspect them in the least. The crisis seemed to have passed, and once again, the halls echoed with talk of the election.

Before going their separate ways to their afternoon classes, Cleo and Robbi decided to meet for the closing of the polls. Something told Cleo she should be around when Mrs. McMillan put away the ballot box at the end of the day.

The reason the vote was left uncounted overnight was because of an old Walton election bylaw, dating from 1798, that permitted students helping their parents with the fall harvest to cast their votes the following morning. Of course, no student had taken advantage of the law in over a hundred years, but at Walton traditions were almost always honored.

After school, Cleo and Robbi hurried to the gym where they watched as the line to vote was cut off at 3:15 and the last student of the day stepped into the booth. Once the boy had dropped his ballot into the box, the two election officials let out a mutual sigh of relief. They were soon joined by several other high school students who helped take the curtains of the booths off their rods and disassemble the skeleton structures. The group packed up pencils and unused ballots and swept up the floor. In no time at all, the gym was back to normal.

"Amazing," said Robbi. "Maybe I can bring these guys home with me to help my dad finish our house."

Cleo didn't answer, she was too busy keeping her eye on the ballot box that had remained in its place on a table.

"Hey, Cleopatra. How's it going?" said the high school girl who had commented on Cleo's name that morning.

"Great," answered Cleo as she shifted her weight uncomfortably. "Is it okay if we stay here for a minute?"

The girl smiled. "Of course. By the way, I'm Megan." She offered her hand.

Cleo took the girl's hand and shook. "Nice to meet you. This is my friend Robbi."

"Nice to meet you, Robbi," said Megan. "I hope you had a chance to vote."

"Sure did," said Robbi.

"Good. It doesn't seem like much, but it's one of the most important things we get to do in this country." She laughed. "Listen to me, I sound like a teacher. Well, anyway, I'd better get back to work. It was good talking to you both."

Cleo and Robbi looked at each other in amazement. They had just had a conversation with an upper school student. Not that they had never talked to any of the high schoolers before, but usually the older kids made the younger ones feel like morons. It was great to be treated with a little respect.

A moment later Mrs. McMillan entered the room. "Hi, kids. Sorry I'm late," she said to the clean-up crew.

"That's all right." "No problem." Everyone echoed similar responses.

Mrs. McMillan walked straight to the table with the ballot box. She didn't comment on the presence of Cleo and Robbi, but did nod her head in their direction, and Cleo thought she might have even smiled.

The headmistress picked up the ballot box and put a long piece of masking tape across the opening. Then she turned the box over. Cleo was shocked to see it was nothing more than a plain cardboard box with a paper towel brand name printed across the sides. She hadn't noticed that this morning. Hard to believe a box that normally would have gone out with the trash held the results of their school election.

Everyone watched as the headmistress checked the remaining sides of the box. When she was satisfied it was secure, she signed her name in several places across the top of the tape, then turned around and nodded at Cleo.

Sure that she had thwarted any would-be ballot switchers, Mrs. McMillan picked up the box, thanked the older students, and walked away.

"No way is Charles going to be able to forge that," whispered Robbi into Cleo's ear.

The girls exchanged a look of relief, happy that Charles wouldn't know about this precaution. It was one more point in their favor.

As the friends bounded away, they failed to notice Michael Payton standing behind the swinging doors. He had seen everything Mrs. McMillan had done to the box and a moment later he hurried out the gym doors on his way to report to Charles.

Chapter 23

Cleo went straight home to pack her trusty overnight bag. If they were going to try to plant the camera and catch Charles in the act they would have to hide out in school for several hours, so Cleo decided to bring along some reading. She didn't think she'd get any studying done with both Robbi and Jason around so she grabbed her pleasure reading from her nightstand. She had been deep into a new mystery/thriller novel but hadn't read one page since the day she had overheard Charles's plan.

She went into her father's office and picked up a big sloppy Columbia sweatshirt from the back of Mr. Oliver's chair. It had been worn thin over the years, but it was just what she needed and she stashed the shirt into her bag. Then she picked her way between stacks of books and boxes until she reached her dad's closet. The door was always left wide open, despite Mrs. Oliver's constant pleas for her husband to keep it closed. Cleo knew in her heart her mom was wasting her time—there was no way her dad's room was ever going to look neat.

On the floor of the closet under a pile of magazines was a medium-sized box that Cleo managed to slide out. Though the box was only the size of a Nintendo set it was extremely heavy because inside were hundreds of keys. None of the keys fit anything important, but Mr. Oliver, the quintessential pack rat, believed he should never throw anything away—let alone something as unique as an old key.

There were keys to hotel rooms he'd never return to, keys to padlocks long lost, keys to a Volvo and other cars that had passed through his life, even keys he'd found on the street—they all had a home in the "key box." Cleo picked out a large ring with four rusty keys on it, then started adding.

When there were thirty keys on the ring, she hefted it in her right hand and shook it. Pleased with both the weight and jingle, Cleo dropped the ring into her bag and put the key box back in the closet.

Her last stop was the kitchen. The teenager opened the large broom closet and borrowed a spray bottle of all-purpose cleaner, two heavy-duty plastic garbage bags, and several of Nortrud's well-used dust rags. Then Cleo headed out the door to Robbi's house.

When she arrived, her friend was sitting on the front stoop. "Where have you been?" demanded Robbi. "Come on, we've got to get the camera."

The two girls went inside the house to the family room on the ground floor. It, too, was still unfinished, though it was strangely inviting. There was a pool table in the center of the room, television set and stereo equipment along one wall, and a mishmash of orientals, navahos, and braided rugs overlapping each other to cover the floor.

Robbi went to the closet in the room and pulled out a small, palm-sized camcorder. "This should hide pretty easily, huh?" she asked Cleo.

Cleo examined the camera and knew right away it would fit nicely between the leaves of Mrs. McMillan's plant. "You know how it works, right?" asked Cleo dubiously.

"Of course," Robbi assured her. "You just press this button and it starts—but wait, we'll need a tape." She reached into a box full of videotapes. "These are all old, but we can tape over them."

"Okay, let's get going," urged Cleo. "I've got another stop to make before we get back to school."

Robbi stuck the camera in its protective bag and packed both it and the tape in her chartreuse and black backpack. "Just let me get my debating notes," said Robbi. "I want to try out some arguments on you guys while we're waiting. I was great today, but we're having another round tomorrow."

"Fine. Just hurry, would you?" Cleo was getting impatient. It was already 4:30.

They made a detour into the Salvation Army Thrift Store on 79th Street. The girls stopped in occasionally because this was one of Robbi's favorite places to shop for clothes. She could satisfy all her kooky tastes here, picking up wild retro clothes from the seventies or hand-painted ties from the fifties.

Right now though, it was Cleo who was busily searching the racks. It didn't take long to find what she was after and, as an unexpected bonus, there was a green tag on the item that meant half off. For two dollars Cleo got a bargain.

As she was paying for it, Robbi showed up at the cash register with a polyester minidress in the most outrageous orange and green print. "I've just got to have this," she said, her eyes gleaming.

"Nice," said Cleo, not really meaning it. She wouldn't be caught dead in anything that ugly. Except as Undercover Cleo . . . well, maybe.

They met Jason at the school gates.

"How did things go at the dentist?" asked Cleo, pretending nothing had happened that morning. "Are you okay?"

"A bit sore, thank you, but otherwise quite fine," he responded. "Anything we need from the outside world? Once we go in, we're in."

The girls looked at each other and shook their heads.

"Then let's have a go at it," said Jason, "before it's too late."

Quite a few other students were still in Walton. There were several special activity clubs that met after school as well as various sports teams that had finished practice and were showering up.

"What's the plan?" asked Robbi, speaking a touch too loudly.

"Keep it down," warned Cleo. "When the gym

empties out, we'll hide under the bleachers. We should be safe there until the school is completely locked up.''

The soccer team was the last to leave the showers and as soon as they were gone the three kids scooted into the gym. There was no sign that the election had even taken place there earlier that day.

The trio went to the far corner of the gym and put their backpacks on the bleachers that were set up on one side.

''Hey,'' said Robbi, ''we should have brought a basketball. Then we could have played a little one-on-one while we wait.''

Cleo and Jason exchanged a look and shook their heads. Robbi really didn't seem to understand the concept of hiding out.

The kids meandered around the room for a few minutes when they heard someone in the hallway. Quickly they grabbed their backpacks and scrambled under the bleachers. They had just scooted themselves into the shadows when Mr. Slovenski burst into the gym, mop and bucket in hand.

''Oh, my gosh,'' whispered Cleo. ''I hope this doesn't mean what I think it means.''

''Just sit still,'' advised Jason. ''Perhaps he won't see us.''

The three kids watched in horror as the custodian walked toward the end of the gym, not far from where they were hiding. He set down the mop, put his arms over his head, and seemed to grow five inches as he stretched out of his hunched-over stance. Then, as he picked up the mop, he shrunk back down again, almost like a cartoon.

Suddenly he looked straight at them. ''Hey, what are

you kids doing in here?'' he yelled. ''Get going. School's out for the day. Go home and bother your parents instead of me.'' He chased the threesome out from under the bleachers, waving his mop menacingly.

Cleo and her friends grabbed their bags and ran for the hall. Behind them they could still hear him sputtering, ''They should wax this floor just once so they can see how hard it is. That'd teach them. Don't they have anything better to do than sit around and watch other people work?''

Out in the hall, the three kids looked at each other in disbelief. ''Now what?'' asked Robbi.

''I guess we pick another room,'' said Cleo. ''I mean, he can't mop the whole school . . . can he?'' She was suddenly worried. This wasn't supposed to happen.

''Down,'' said Jason. The three kids went down a flight of stairs to the fifth floor where they tried the door to the library. It was locked so they went along the hall trying the doors to all the classrooms. Robbi found one open, and they rushed in after her and squeezed behind a bookcase, pulling their bags in under their knees.

''He definitely can't see us here,'' said Robbi, poking her head out to check.

''Not unless he decides to mop the place,'' replied Jason. ''But I'd say we're okay.''

''Don't get too comfortable,'' warned Cleo. ''Not that that's possible.'' There wasn't much room behind the bookcase and even though they had just been chased out of the gym, it wasn't long before all three were relaxing and stretching out their legs.

"How long do you think we'll have to wait here?" asked Robbi.

"Until Mr. Slovenski leaves," replied Jason. "We-'ve got to be sure we're the only ones in the building before we go sneaking about."

Robbi sighed, then brightened. "Well, then, do you guys want to hear my arguments for tomorrow's debate?"

She had no sooner pulled out her index cards when the kids heard Mr. Slovenski in the hall singing an off-key version of "Blue Suede Shoes."

Robbi started giggling but squelched it when she saw Cleo staring her down. "I'm sorry, but that's about the worst thing I've ever heard," Robbi whispered. "Talk about tone deaf."

"What's he doing, besides making me really nerv-ous?" Cleo said under her breath. "Doesn't he ever go home?"

The kids pulled themselves back into tight clumps as they waited for the custodian to pass. Instead they heard the man's singing stop and there was a jingle of keys just down the hall.

"What's happening?" asked Cleo, a feeling of alarm crawling over her back.

"Not to worry, I'll check it out," Jason reassured her. "Oh, have either of you got a small mirror?"

Cleo took her mirror from her bag and handed it to the boy, who crawled toward the door. The second he reached it, a door slammed loudly down the hall and Jason flattened himself against the floor while the girls stifled screams and clutched onto each other.

When his hand stopped shaking, Jason held up the mirror. The room they were in was at the end of the hall and when he held up the small glass he would see down the length of the corridor. Cleo and Robbi watched Jason's face as he angled the mirror to get the proper view. His eyebrows raised, then scrunched, and in no time at all, he was sliding back across the floor on his hands and knees. "Come on, we've got to get out of here," he said frantically.

"Why?" asked Cleo, trying not to shout.

"Because that man is checking every room and locking them up, one by one."

The kids grabbed their bags and hurried to the door. When Jason saw Mr. Slovenski step into the classroom next door, he nodded to the girls. The three of them raced out the door and into the hallway. After a moment of confusion, they all ran to the stairwell and quickly ran down, wanting to put as much distance between them and the custodian as possible.

They were now on the fourth floor and searching desperately for another hiding place. Soon Mr. Slovenski would have locked every room on the fifth floor and would be doing the same on the fourth. It was only a matter of time until they ended up trapped in the basement. The three kids darted into the music room, looking around, but they knew it was no use and Jason was starting to panic.

"We can't just keep running and hiding in different rooms," Jason said. "Sooner or later, he'll have locked up everything and we'll be stuck with no place to hide. What are we going to do?"

"Maybe we should just go home," suggested Robbi. "We could call Mrs. McMillan tonight and . . ."

"You know we can't do that," scolded Cleo. "Come on, we've gotten this far, we can't give up now."

Jason nodded but Cleo could see that he wasn't very happy with the situation. Robbi, on the other hand, was starting to get excited. This was just the kind of adventure her thrill-seeking nature thrived on.

"Maybe we should hide in the air ducts," she suggested. She had seen it happen in lots of movies and it seemed so simple.

"I don't think so," said Cleo. She pointed upward. "Do you see any air vents?"

"This building's too old," said Jason. "Nice try though, Rob." The praise sounded genuine, but Robbi still regarded him suspiciously.

"I've got an idea," said Cleo. "Why do we have to keep going down? Mr. Slovenski's already locked up the sixth floor. He won't go back up there so even though we'd have to sit in the hallway, he won't see us. Our only problem right now is to get into Mrs. McMillan's office. You two go on up. When Mr. Slovenski goes into the next classroom, head up to the sixth floor. I'll meet you in a little while." Robbi nodded her head and started for the door, but Jason didn't move.

"I'm afraid I don't quite understand what your plan is," he said.

Robbi yanked the boy away. "Trust me, she can handle it. Come on. We've got to run." She checked the hallway, then pulled the boy out of the music room and up the stairs before he could ask any more questions.

Cleo watched her friends disappear before ducking into the girls' rest room. A moment later she heard the off-key singing once again as Mr. Slovenski arrived on the fourth floor and began locking up.

In a frenzy Cleo unpacked her black bag. She worked as fast as she could, using the techniques of an undercover agent, and in a matter of seconds she had stippled freckles on her face using a textured sponge. Moments later she had slapped on black kohl liner around her eyes, applied a bright royal-blue mascara, and put on garish orange lipstick. Cleo then tied a bandanna on her head, sweatband style, slipped her father's large sweatshirt on over her own shirt, and pulled on the red acid-washed jeans that had been her two-dollar purchase at the thrift store.

In only three minutes Cleo had given herself yet another character's face and added several pounds to her slim frame. Pulling out the two plastic garbage bags she'd brought from home, she put one inside the other, doubling the thickness, and stuffed her overnight bag into them.

Then Cleo stepped back to check her disguise in the mirror, but in her hurry, she knocked the bag off the sink. The clunk scared her as much as it did Mr. Slovenski who was passing by just outside the door. His tone-deaf singing cut off in the middle of a horribly wrong note.

The custodian banged on the door as he shouted, "Who's in there? Come on out, you hear me!"

Chapter 24

Undercover Cleo bunched the top of the garbage bag together in her hand and pushed her way out through the swinging door. By the time she stepped into the hallway, she had become "Julie" the cleaning girl.

"Julie" had rags and a spray cleaner bottle tucked in her belt and she dragged a plastic trash bag behind her. She glared at Mr. Slovenski and chomped on a huge wad of gum, not bothering to keep her mouth shut as she chewed. "Excuse me, but is this or is this not the *ladies'* room," she said, giving the man plenty of what her father termed "bad-itude." "Can't a person fix her hair without being disturbed?" Cleo had teased and sprayed her bangs so that they stood four inches above her head.

"Who are you?" asked the custodian. "You don't work here."

"Don't I wish," sassed "Julie." She stood in an exaggerated version of Cleo's own slouch, projecting the image of a young, quasi-lazy working girl. "I'm Julie, and don't tell me, you're Slovenski, right? My sister's told me all about you."

"Your sister?" asked the man, clearly suspicious.

"Jessie? Jessie Moss?" Cleo knew Jessie Moss worked part-time at Walton as a cleaning woman. "She's sick today. Asked me to fill in. And boy, am I glad she did. I'm having *such* a good time." Undercover Cleo's tone was dripping with sarcasm.

Mr. Slovenski stared at Cleo for a long moment before saying, "That Jessie's always sick. You tell her next time she's got to check with me before she sends somebody new to do her job. Well, don't just stand there, get to work."

"Yeah, well, that's what I was trying to do," huffed Undercover Cleo. She started off down the hall, then turned back. "Oh, by the way, I think I, uh, you know, like locked my keys in one of the rooms downstairs. Could you maybe open it for me?"

Mr. Slovenski growled, but accompanied "Julie" downstairs. "Okay, but only if you stop popping that blasted gum," he complained. "What a disgusting habit."

Undercover Cleo blew another bubble just for effect, and stared back at Mr. Slovenski when he whirled and glared at her. "Sor-ry," she mouthed off.

This is really kind of fun, Cleo thought. *I can say and do all sorts of things when I'm Undercover Cleo.*

"Julie" led the way down the staircase until the twosome reached the main floor, then she began looking around in confusion. "Um, now I'm not sure which room it was. Maybe this one." Undercover Cleo headed toward Mr. Allen's office. As Mr. Slovenski followed the girl, he hunted on his giant key ring until he had the key he needed to open the door.

"Oh, no, it wasn't this one," the cleaning girl said. "Boy, these doors all look the same, don't they?"

The custodian let forth a loud growl of exasperation, but Cleo ignored him and kept busy snapping her gum and studying the long hallway of doors. She wanted to keep the man off balance and well away from her two friends upstairs.

"It must have been that room," "Julie " said as she walked across the hall.

"That's a faculty bathroom. You left your keys in the bathroom? Have you wasted time fixing your hair on every floor? Anyway, it's unlocked. You don't need me," reprimanded Mr. Slovenski as he turned to leave.

"Oh. Well, then it must be this one here," said "Julie," " 'cause I definitely locked them in." Cleo went to Mrs. McMillan's office and rattled the door-knob, finding it locked as she knew it would be. "Yeah, this is the one." Undercover Cleo stepped back and stared at the custodian, behaving as if she were doing the man a huge favor, though in reality she was very worried that her ploy might not work. "I'm waiting, Slovenski. Or are we supposed to be doing this by magic?"

Mr. Slovenski was completely taken aback by this smart-talking substitute cleaning girl. Almost everyone gave him a wide berth, though he knew they made fun of him behind his back. For the past forty years he had managed to keep both students and staff a little afraid of him, but he rarely faced off against anyone with the chutzpah of Jessie Moss's sister. This girl was sassing him at every opportunity.

Normally he would have given her a piece of his mind, but he was tired after doing those floors upstairs and what he wanted now, more than anything else, was for Julie to go away. So without another thought, he unlocked the door to Mrs. McMillan's office.

The substitute cleaning woman slouched her way into the room, looked around, and tilted her head back like it was too heavy for her neck. "Yeah, this is it. I'm sure they're here somewhere," said Undercover Cleo. She shuffled over to Ms. Appleby's desk, then made her way behind it. Bending down, Cleo reached into her pocket and pulled out the set of keys she had assembled from her father's key box. Then she held them up triumphantly to show Mr. Slovenski.

"I knew it," she said. "You didn't believe me, did you, Slovenski?" Undercover Cleo jiggled the keys in his face.

"Not believe a pea brain like you would lose her keys? Of course I believed you," countered the man. "And stop rattling those things." He looked around the office. "By the way, I don't know if your sister filled you in on this part of your job, but you're supposed to *clean* these offices before you lock them up. Look at the dust on those shelves and the fingerprints on the door. Do this room again and you'd better make sure you do the rest of the rooms on this floor, too." Feeling that he was back in control, the custodian allowed himself a smirk of victory.

Undercover Cleo nodded her head. "Right. Like I have time to clean every room twice."

The custodian gave "Julie" his most severe look that quickly changed the girl's thinking.

"Okay, fine. Have it your way," she said, pulling her dust rag from her belt and lackadaisically running it over the desk. To push his buttons a little more, Cleo took a headset from her fannypack, put it over her ears, and proceeded to blow a final humongous bubble. When it burst with a loud *pop*, she turned and flashed her brattiest smile.

The man glared at "Julie," then left the room mumbling to himself. Cleo peeked out the window of the office door and watched him disappear up the stairwell.

I can't believe he fell for that, she thought. But there wasn't any time to pat herself on the back. Knowing Robbi and Jason had to be uncomfortable waiting out in the open, Cleo was anxious to get her friends safely into Mrs. McMillan's office.

She wadded a small piece of paper into a ball, then stuffed it into the slot in the door frame where the door locked. *That ought to get us back in,* Cleo thought, and tested her improvised system from the inside just to be sure.

"Yes!" It was exhilarating to see the door pop open. Cleo went out, carefully shutting the door behind her, then darted up the big winding stairwell.

She took the stairs three at a time, only slowing down when she hit the fourth floor and heard the custodian serenading again—this time a weird tune that kept slipping back and forth between "Easter Bonnet" and "Hark! The Herald Angels Sing." Peeking out onto the corridor, she saw the man come out of a classroom, then lock the door. When he entered the next room, Cleo continued her dash up the stairs.

"Robbi, Jason, get down to Mrs. McMillan's office on the double," she whispered into the sixth-floor hallway. She kept herself hidden in the stairwell, not wanting Jason to see her dressed up as "Julie." When she heard her friends scrambling toward her, she turned and hurried down to the fifth floor.

Cleo took a rag and started polishing a locker, keeping an eye on the stairwell. In less than a minute, she saw Robbi and Jason sneak down. Just before they disappeared, Jason turned and looked out onto the floor, staring straight at Cleo.

Startled, the girl looked away and began scrubbing the metal even more vigorously. She knew her disguise was great, but the way he was scrutinizing her was nerve-wracking.

When she peeked again, her friends were gone. All that was left now was for her to get out of costume and into the office with her friends.

She started descending the stairs, listening for the whereabouts of the custodian. *He must be on the third floor, maybe even the second now,* she thought. She peered out onto the corridor of the third floor and seeing it empty, continued her trek down, but in the few seconds it took to pass the level, Mr. Slovenski came out of the room he had been in and saw Julie on her way to the second floor.

"Hey, you! Get back over here!" he called.

Undercover Cleo froze, then slowly she turned around and walked back up the steps.

"Yeah?" she answered.

The custodian had decided he'd have to do something about this nuisance of a girl. No one took advantage of Leon Slovenski. No one.

Walking over to her, he growled, "What are you doing running around up here? I thought I left you to clean the rooms on the first floor. You can't have done the lunchroom yet. Get back down there and do the job right! And be sure everything's locked up when you're done."

With a yawn, Undercover Cleo picked up her trash bag and dragged it through the hall. "Fine," she said. "But I'm outta here right after that. Can't say it's been a real pleasure, you know."

"Julie" knew Mr. Slovenski was watching so she dawdled all the way down the stairs.

The way things had been going so far, she was expecting to see the wad of paper on the ground outside Mrs. McMillan's office and her friends standing in the hall in total panic. To her relief, the hall was empty.

Cleo ducked into the auditorium and quickly changed back to herself. She stripped off the extra clothing, brushed down her hair and wiped off the makeup, and stuffed everything back into her bag. After making sure the coast was clear, she made a beeline for the office. When she pushed the door, it opened and she slipped inside.

"Anyone here?" she whispered as she took the wad of paper out of the lock slot in the door frame.

"Over here," came Robbi's voice and her grinning face bobbed up from behind Ms. Appleby's desk. Jason's head rose slowly behind her.

"Where were you?" he asked Cleo.

"I, uh . . . wanted to get something out of my locker," Cleo lied.

Jason didn't appear to believe her entirely, but he didn't ask any more questions.

"Listen, how do we know Mr. Slovenski won't check in here before locking up?"

Jason's question started butterflies in Cleo's stomach as she realized it was entirely possible that the custodian would stop by to check on "Julie's" sloppy work. Cleo knew she hadn't exactly inspired the man's confidence in her cleaning abilities, but she didn't dare worry her friends now.

"I know we're safe because I heard Mr. Slovenski telling the cleaning woman to take care of this floor. I followed her down and stuck the paper in the door when she was dusting, but it wouldn't hurt us to have our hiding places ready." Cleo was pleased to see that her answer seemed to satisfy the boy.

The kids went into Mrs. McMillan's inner office and gathered behind the headmistress's desk.

"I certainly hope this is worth it," said Jason. "I feel like a prowler."

"Then leave, Jason," said Robbi. "But Charles will win if you do, and not just because he's switching the ballots, but because you're not doing anything about it. That'd make you a two-time loser."

"And if I get caught sneaking about school grounds after hours, I'll be an even bigger loser," he said, making his point.

"Come on," said Robbi, "we've already stopped Charles once today, we can do it again. . . . " The girl's words trailed off as she realized she had just let the cat out of the bag.

"What do you mean?" Jason asked.

Cleo shot her friend the dirtiest look she had. "She doesn't mean anything," she told Jason. "Look, we'd better get the camera in place while we have a chance and then we've got to find some hiding places."

"All right," said Jason, agreeing to continue the plan.

Robbi took the small camcorder out of her bag and walked to the potted plant. "Here, right?" she asked. "This is great. No one'll see it under all these leaves." She jammed it between some branches.

Jason looked through the viewfinder. "Oh, excellent, Robbi. It's perfectly placed to videotape the leaves. That'll impress Mrs. McMillan to no end."

"So I'm a debater not a photographer," said Robbi, sticking out her tongue at the boy behind his back.

Jason adjusted the position of the camera and widened out the zoom lens until the angle of view covered the critical area of the room. Then he carefully rearranged the leaves of the plant to hide the body of the camera.

"Isn't there a light that goes on when it's recording?" asked Cleo.

"Good thinking," answered Jason. "It's right out in front here and someone might very easily have noticed it." He took a piece of paper from his notebook, colored it black with his pen, then used a piece of Scotch tape from Mrs. McMillan's desk to secure it over the tiny red bulb. "There, that ought to do it."

"We should turn it on fifteen or twenty minutes before eight," suggested Cleo. "I mean, in case Charles happens to show up early."

"Righto," said Jason. "And now we've got to find hiding places."

"How about the other closet?" asked Cleo. "Maybe we can squeeze in there." She walked over and opened it. Inside were a few empty coat hangers and an extra pair of Mrs. McMillan's clunky black shoes.

Cleo picked up the shoes and moved them to the upper shelf in the closet.

"I don't know, it looks a bit tight," said Jason.

"Let's see if we can squeeze in," said Robbi, who clearly thought the idea was going to be loads of fun.

Jason went first, pushing himself all the way back into a corner of the closet. Cleo went next, then Robbi tried to shove herself in on top of them.

"Wow, it's gonna be cramped," she said, still half out of the closet. Cleo was smushed up against Jason so close she was getting embarrassed.

"A little *too* cramped, Rob," said Cleo. "There's no

way that we're all gonna fit in here.''

"Sure we will.'' Robbi shoved and pushed harder but no matter how she tried, she couldn't jam herself in with the other two, not if she wanted to shut the closet door.

"Okay, Robbi, enough. It won't work,'' said Cleo. Robbi's antics were squeezing Cleo and Jason into pancakes.

"Maybe one of us could hide under the desk?'' Robbi suggested.

"I don't think that would be wise,'' said Jason. "What if Charles or one of his friends happens to sit back there?''

Cleo started examining the room again. There didn't seem to be any place to hide. Unless . . . She walked to the long, low metal filing cabinet and opened the top drawer. It was full of papers, but the bottom drawer was empty.

"Well, what do you guys think?'' she asked. "Someone might get in here. Someone small.'' She and Jason both looked at Robbi at the same moment.

"Oh, thanks a whole lot,'' retorted Robbi. "That does not exactly look comfortable.''

But to Robbi's great dismay, once she had been convinced to climb into the drawer, she fit perfectly. It was obvious there was no way the drawer would work for either Jason or Cleo.

After they closed the drawer with Robbi in it, she commented from within, "Now I know how a sardine feels.''

Cleo hid a smile—sometimes it wasn't so bad being

tall. She pulled the drawer open again and tried making her friend feel better. "I'm sure you won't have to be in there too long."

"Not more than several hours," teased Jason.

"You'd better get out for now," said Cleo. "We've still got a lot of time before Charles shows up."

Their hiding places ready, the kids had nothing to do but wait. They wandered around the office, browsing through the books on Mrs. McMillan's shelves and looking at pictures on her desk, when they heard Mr. Slovenski's rendition of "Feelings."

"Quick. Behind the desk," said Cleo. The three kids scrambled into place.

"He must be going home for the day," whispered Cleo, trying to reassure her friends as well as herself. "A few more minutes and we'll have the place to ourselves." But instead of the song disappearing through the front gates, it got louder and louder until it stopped right outside the office.

"I'm sure that noodlehead girl didn't clean a darn thing in here," the man mumbled loudly.

Cleo, Robbi, and Jason looked at each other in terror as they heard the keys at the door.

Chapter 25

"Into the drawer!" cried Cleo.

"There's no time," said Robbi, pushing Jason and Cleo toward the closet. "Now just stay put." She made sure her friends were safely hidden before running out into Ms. Appleby's area of the office. Clasping her hands around the doorknob, she pulled and yelled, "Help, let me out!"

"What is she doing?" whispered Jason.

Cleo knew her friend better than anyone, and *she* had no idea what Robbi was up to.

"What? Who's in there?" asked the custodian. "Just hold your horses while I get it unlocked."

A second later he opened the door and Robbi burst out into the hall. "Thanks, Mr. Slovenski. You saved my life. I was leaving after my chess club meeting and I saw Mrs. McMillan's door wide open." Robbi hung her head as she continued, "I figured she was here and I wanted to ask her something and then somebody locked the door behind me."

"That scatterbrained Julie," the man said, shaking his head. "Don't worry, she won't be working around here again."

"I'm so glad you came by," said Robbi, "I thought for sure I would have to spend the night in there."

Mr. Slovenski studied the girl who seemed truly upset, and all at once he softened. She was so relieved and—could it be?—even glad to see him, and that wasn't an everyday occurrence. Usually the kids cleared out of the way when they saw him coming. He patted the small girl on the shoulder.

"Are you all right, honey?" he asked.

"Yeah, I was pretty scared, but I'm okay now. I just want to go home," said Robbi, sniffling a little and rubbing her eyes.

"I'll walk you out," said Mr. Slovenski, who, in his concern for the girl, forgot all about checking the room. He escorted her across the courtyard and to the street. When he was sure she would be all right walking home alone, he turned back to the school, put a heavy chain and lock on the iron gates, then clipped his keys back onto his belt loop. As he turned to head for home, he saw Robbi Richards skipping down the street, without so much as a backward glance at Walton.

In the office Jason and Cleo climbed out of the closet.

"Robbi is definitely a candidate for the loony bin," said Cleo.

"Certifiable," said Jason.

"But she sure did save our butts just now," said Cleo, who knew how much it had meant to Robbi to be in on this adventure. The fact that she'd sacrificed it made Cleo love her friend all the more.

"Yes, well, too bad she's no longer in the game, but I suppose we must carry on as planned," said Jason. His statement actually came out as a question.

"Oh, yeah, of course. We can't leave now. Robbi would want us to see it through," Cleo assured the boy.

Just then Cleo realized she would be spending the next few *hours* alone in the room with Jason. All her insecurities came flooding back, and suddenly she was painfully aware of the four-inch-height difference between herself and the boy. In a move she had perfected, Cleo pulled a book out of her bag and plopped down on the floor behind the desk. Sitting was always a quick equalizer.

"I thought I'd get in a little reading since we have such a long wait," she said, burying her face in the text.

"Oh, right," Jason agreed though he sounded slightly disappointed. He opened his pack and found his algebra book.

Cleo was so busy watching Jason out of the corner of her eye that it took her ten minutes to read one paragraph. She wondered if math was hard for him, or if he was also having a hard time concentrating because it seemed to take him forever to do one problem. Finally, after a few more minutes, Jason coughed.

"You know I could still lose the election," he

started, "but at least I'll know I lost fairly. I won't mind losing that way at all. Well, at least not too much." He smiled. "I have you to thank, Cleo Oliver."

"Uh, you're welcome," said Cleo. To her surprise, Jason moved next to her. She knew she was beginning to blush so she stared down into her lap hoping Jason wouldn't notice.

They talked for a little while about nothing in particular, until Jason looked straight at Cleo and said, "I'm also glad I'm getting to know you."

Cleo felt a mammoth heat wave spread out across her body. She knew she ought to say that she was glad to know Jason, but she didn't trust her voice not to crack, so she took a moment to swallow. She was just ready to lift her head and say something noncommittal like "I only wanted to help," or "I would have done the same for anyone," when a soft knock at the door interrupted her.

Jason and Cleo froze for a heartbeat, then quietly ducked down and crept under the desk. They were hoping whoever it was would go away and had just pulled themselves in when the knock came again, this time louder and more insistent.

"Open up, guys. It's me," came a voice.

Cleo and Jason looked at each other in surprise.

"It's Robbi," said Cleo, and she scrambled to her feet. Running in a crouch, Cleo got to the door and opened it to see Robbi standing in the doorway—holding a pizza!

"Took you long enough," Robbi reprimanded her friend.

Cleo was incredulous. "But how . . . ?" She didn't get a chance to finish the question before Robbi handed her the large flat box.

"Take this, would you? My fingers are burning." Robbi blew on her fingertips, then reached in her pockets for a glob of napkins.

Jason appeared behind Cleo. "Will you two close the door before Mr. Slovenski comes back." He pulled the girls inside and quietly shut the door behind them.

"Get a grip," said Robbi. "Slovenski's definitely gone. In fact, he even walked me out of the front gates. We're absolutely alone in this place for the next two hours." She pompously strode in to Mrs. McMillan's desk. "I thought we should all have some dinner."

"Robbi Richards, answer me," demanded Cleo. "How did you get back in?"

Robbi decided to be annoying, something she was very good at. "Hmm. That might just have to be one of *my* secrets." She opened the box of pizza and selected a slice, dripping with cheese. "Mmmmm," she sighed, taking a bite. "Delivering pizza makes a person hungry."

"Rob-bi . . ." Cleo was growing impatient.

The small girl laughed. "Okay, okay. You know when I was poking around in Mr. Slovenski's room last week?"

Cleo and Jason nodded.

"I noticed a window in there that faces out onto the back alley. It was open, I mean, it was actually rusted

open, but I sort of checked it out while I was in there."
Robbi was smug about her accomplishment. "It's really, really small, but *I* managed to squeeze through with the pizza."

"You see what I mean," Cleo said to Jason. "She's definitely crazy." But she was happy her friend had made it back, especially with dinner. Cleo reached for a slice, being careful not to let the cheese ooze onto the floor.

Jason also took a piece of the cheese pie and between the three of them, the pizza vanished in record time. Besides the fact that it was past dinnertime, the three kids had worked up a serious appetite running up and down the stairwells. After they finished, the teenagers shared a few moments of contented silence, then they folded the box, stuffed it in a small garbage can under Mrs. McMillan's desk, and cleaned up as well as they could.

"It's a quarter to eight," said Cleo, looking at her watch. "Charles said something about an eight o'clock movie being their alibi." Suddenly everyone was nervous all over again. They packed up their bags and put them on the shelf in the closet where Cleo and Jason would be hiding.

"Make sure you don't forget anything," warned Jason. "We can't afford for this to go wrong now."

Jason and Cleo packed a grumbling Robbi into her drawer, making sure she was securely in place. Then they checked the view of the camera one last time and turned it on.

"Be sure you stay out of the picture," warned Jason.

The two kids stayed at the sides of the room as they crept to the closet.

"How do we know Charles won't open this door first?" asked Cleo. She hated to bring up the problem, but it had to be done.

"Good golly," said Jason. "I never thought of that. I just assumed he would know it was the other closet like we did, since it's the one with the lock. But I suppose there's always a chance he'll open ours first, isn't there?"

Cleo nodded fearfully.

The boy studied the inside of the closet door, then chuckled. "I've got it," he said, taking two coat hangers off of the rod.

Cleo watched as he opened them up, then twisted them together tightly, forming one long wire. Next he secured one end around the coat rod, being sure that it couldn't be pulled off. "Come on, then," he said to her. "Climb in."

Cleo looked at the boy quizzically, but he only motioned for her to step in. Once they were both inside, she watched as he twisted the other end tightly around the inner door handle. In order to open the door now, a person would have to yank hard enough to pull the whole hanging rod down as well.

"Locked in," Jason said proudly. "It may not hold if Charles really wants to get in, but it should be enough of a hindrance to get him to try the other closet first. We can both feel a bit safer now."

"Great going," said Cleo. She did feel a little more

at ease knowing that Charles wasn't likely to discover them hiding in the office.

It was tight quarters and Cleo tried to keep a little space between Jason and herself, but she only managed to hold the position for a few minutes before she felt a cramp coming on. Reluctantly she had to relax and she felt her shoulder make contact with the boy. A moment later she realized it would be better if she breathed as well. She took in a big gulp of air that, to her horror, turned into a hiccup.

Trying to hold the hiccups in, Cleo felt her whole body jerk. Then, being nervous, she started giggling uncontrollably. Jason joined in a moment later, and the two were convulsed in laughter until they heard voices and the sound of keys in the hall.

Chapter 26

The next sound was Charles's voice. "We're in, guys, let's go. From here on in, it's a breeze. Am I brilliant or what?"

"I think we should hurry up, okay?" said Andy, his nervousness apparent in his voice.

"No, Monahan, I was thinking of staying here all night," said Charles sarcastically. "Of course, we're gonna hurry."

Cleo was grateful that her hiccups had been scared right out of her, but now she found there was a tickle in her throat and she needed to swallow. The situation was much more frightening than she could ever have imagined. She started gagging, until Jason patted her reassuringly on the arm. Finally, after what seemed like a year, Cleo calmed herself down enough to do a slow swallow.

Cleo and Jason watched the beam of a flashlight flit past the crack at the bottom of their closet door. Luckily it didn't rest there but went on, presumably to the other locked door.

"Which closet is it?" asked Charles.

"The one on the right," said Michael. He had been so quiet that Cleo hadn't been sure he'd even come along.

"Gimme those keys," Charles said and once again there was the tinkle of keys.

"Hey," said Andy. "Am I nuts or does it smell like pizza in here?" He started looking around the room. "Guys, get this. There's a Pizza Palace box in the trash. Old McMillan must have downed a whole pie. Incredible."

"Will you shut up?" said Michael.

Cleo could hear the sound of keys as Charles tried one after another in the lock.

"What's the matter, Maxwell?" asked Andy. He sat on top of the low filing cabinet where Robbi was hiding and began nervously banging his heels on the metal sides. Andy was only a foot away from the potted plant and the camera.

Inside the drawer Robbi gritted her teeth. The metal amplified the sound and each kick was like a cannon going off beside her head. She thought she'd be lucky if she had any hearing left at all after this.

"Put a lid on the noise, Monahan," said Michael. "People can hear that in the next state. Maxwell, what is taking you so long?"

Andy stopped kicking while Charles continued

patiently with the key ring. Then he hit the winning key. "Yabba dabba doo," he said in triumph. "Boys, we're almost home."

Charles carefully lifted the cardboard box from the closet and carried it to the desk. "Just like you said, Payton—Old Lady McMillan signed the tape. But of course, we have come prepared."

Michael walked over to the desk alongside Charles and examined the box. From their hiding places, Cleo and her friends listened, trying to decipher what was going on.

Charles made himself comfortable in Mrs. McMillan's chair and arranged the ballot box in front of him. He flipped it over, took a razor blade, and cut the bottom of the box along the seam where it had been glued. He was very careful not to tear the cardboard. "This is a piece of cake. Good thing McMillan didn't tape around the whole box though." He looked up at his pal. "Payton, you did bring the glue, didn't you?" he asked.

Michael nodded his head, dug in his bag, and handed Charles a bottle of white school glue and some paper towels to clean up.

"I don't think I want to see this," said Andy, suddenly jumping off his perch. "I'm outta here." He headed for the door.

Charles was out of the chair in a flash and grabbed Andy by the back of his black jacket. "Whoa there, boy. No one's going anywhere until we're done. Capisce?"

"You said we weren't going to have to break in here

and switch the votes," complained Andy. "You said you'd changed your mind, that all we had to do was put Fleming's test in Garrett's backpack and that would take care of the whole election."

Charles led Andy back to his place on the filing cabinet. "Yeah, well, I thought it would work but it didn't," he said. "How was I supposed to know Garrett would find out and ditch the papers before they searched his bag? You know, I still can't figure out how that guy caught on. Anyway, just shut up right now so I can do this, okay?"

In the shadows of the closet, Jason gave Cleo a nudge and a questioning look. She averted her eyes and did her best to put on an innocent face.

Charles finished working open the bottom of the box, then dumped the ballots out into a plastic trash bag he had brought just for this purpose. He looked up and grinned at his buddies before pulling out another plastic bag from his backpack. This one was full of the ballots he had marked himself that afternoon confirming his landslide victory over Jason Garrett. Without hesitation, Charles poured the phony ballots into the open bottom of the box. "Glue," he called out, sounding like a surgeon on a television show.

He took the offered bottle from Michael and meticulously spread the adhesive into the seam. He pressed down the flaps and carefully wiped off the excess before looking up again.

"That's it, we're gonna rule this year," said Andy, apparently not feeling as confident as he sounded, because he immediately resumed kicking the filing cabinet.

Charles double-checked the bottom of the box. "The glue will be dry by morning and McMillan will never in a million years notice it's been opened. All we've got to do is get rid of those," he said, pointing to the bag of real ballots.

"No problem," said Andy. He jumped off the cabinet, took the plastic bag in his hand, and dumped it into the trash can under Mrs. McMillan's desk, pushing it down on top of the pizza box.

"Oh, real smart, Monahan," Charles snarled, "just shove them in McMillan's face, why don't you? We *destroy* the evidence, remember? In the furnace."

Charles leaned over and grabbed the bag of ballots from the wastepaper basket. "These stay in my locker tonight. First thing tomorrow, when the heat comes on, I take them down to the basement and have the great pleasure of watching them burn."

Cleo had overheard the boys plotting on two other occasions, but this time everything seemed much worse, probably because they were in the room actually in the process of committing the crime. Jason seemed just as disturbed as Cleo and quietly took her hand and squeezed it. Cleo squeezed back and slightly shifted her position. In doing so, she bumped a hanger off the pole in the closet. The clatter scared every one of the six of the kids in the office.

"Let's get out of here," said Andy, already halfway to the door.

"Wait a minute. We gotta see what that was,"

Charles told his friends. "Come on, you're not chicken, are you?"

"What if it's a rat or something, Maxwell?" asked Michael. His voice sounded pretty close to the door, too.

"We're going to check this out," commanded Charles.

Jason and Cleo watched as the beam of the flashlight danced around the edges of their closet door. Cleo closed her eyes in terror and stood frozen while Jason tightened his grip on her hand.

Chapter 27

Just then a fire truck, its siren screeching, blasted past the school. It wasn't an unusual happening in New York City, but the sound made the neck hairs stand up on the three boys.

"That's it, good-bye," said Andy.

"Yeah, come on, Maxwell," said Michael. "Anyway, I'm starving. That pizza smells too good."

"Okay, fine. If it'll make you crybabies feel better, let's go," agreed Charles, not willing to admit he was spooked himself. He picked up the ballot box off the desk and returned it to the closet.

Cleo and Jason listened to the click as Charles locked the closet, then the slam of the office door as the three boys made a quick exit.

No one dared to move until several minutes had passed, then Jason quickly untwisted his makeshift coat-hanger lock. Seconds later he and Cleo wrangled themselves out of the closet. It felt great to be out of the hiding place and they were both stretching their arms and legs when they were startled by a loud banging.

It was Robbi inside the filing cabinet. "Come on, you guys, get me out of here! Let me out!"

Still mindful of the camcorder, Cleo and Jason crawled to the cabinet. While the boy reached up to take care of the camera, Cleo pulled the bottom drawer open. She couldn't help laughing at the exasperated expression on her friend's face.

"That was sheer torture," Robbi complained. "Can you believe Andy Monahan, kicking like that the whole time? I'm going to have to order a Miracle Ear." She crawled out of the drawer and looked down at it. "At least a coffin has padding."

Jason was busy with the camcorder. "Let's hope everything came out okay on the tape." He opened the cartridge and slid out the tape.

Cleo was taking their backpacks off of the closet shelf when Jason moaned.

"Who put this tape in the camera?" he asked.

Robbi apprehensively answered, "I did. Why? What's the matter?"

Jason held up the tape. Cleo and Robbi looked at the cassette and then at each other, not understanding.

"I don't get it," said Cleo.

"Look here," Jason said, pointing to the back of the tape. "See this square hole, it's supposed to have a little plastic tab in it. When it's broken out, it means you can't record over it, unless you cover the hole again. Whatever was on this tape when we came in is still there.'' Jason groaned and slumped onto the cabinet top. ''All this work for nothing.''

Robbi was horrified. ''I'm so sorry. I didn't know, really.'' She hung her head.

''Don't worry,'' Cleo spoke up. ''We've got everything we need.'' She was actually smiling.

Her friends looked at her, completely confused by Cleo's confident air.

''Whatever do you mean?'' asked Jason finally.

Cleo stuck her hand in her pocket and pulled out a small black device. ''Voilà,'' she cried.

Seeing her friends didn't understand, she explained. ''It's my father's microcassette recorder. We've got everything that was said on tape. It's only audio tape, but that should still do the trick. The Three Stooges mentioned each other's names several times and anybody should be able to tell that it's them. It's something I learned from my dad—always have a backup system.''

She quickly rewound the tape a little, listening for the moment when the three boys made their exit. Cleo wanted to erase everything said after the boys had left. It was vital that neither she nor her friends could be heard on the tape.

Once Cleo was satisfied that only Charles's, Andy's, and Michael's voices were on the tape, she triumphantly popped the small cassette out of the recorder. With a smile to Robbi and Jason, she pulled a white envelope from her bag, then placed the tape inside.

Then she printed, again using her left hand, DEAR MRS. MCMILLAN, PLEASE LISTEN TO THIS BEFORE YOU COUNT THE VOTES.

Cleo set the envelope in the middle of Mrs. Mc-Millan's desk, grabbed her black bag, and looked around, her eyes making a final sweep of the room. Then, silently, the trio walked out into the hall.

They headed down the corridor, straight for a side door that led to 76th Street. The three kids waited until the coast was clear, then quickly went out the door, making sure it was securely shut behind them. It was only 8:30, but they were all exhausted. They said quiet good-byes, split up, and headed for their respective homes.

Cleo let herself into the apartment and went straight to her room. She didn't feel like answering any questions about her day, no matter how innocent. She opened the secret drawer in her bed and found her journal. The events of the day just had to be written down. It had been one of the most exciting days of her whole life.

After Cleo had made her entry, she put the journal back in its place. Then, sublimely satisfied with her accomplishments, she fell into a deep and dreamless sleep.

Chapter 28

At precisely 7:45 in the morning, as Mrs. McMillan did on almost every school day, she walked briskly into her office. "Good morning, Alice," she said to her assistant. "Give me a few minutes and I'll be ready to count the vote."

"Just buzz me," replied Ms. Appleby, "and I'll be right in."

The headmistress had a lot to do this morning and immediately began making notes to herself on her microrecorder. When she noticed the envelope on her desk, she clicked off the small machine and set it down. She was certain that she'd cleared off her desk the night before and her suspicions were immediately aroused. On top of that, there was a lingering odor of pizza in the air.

"Alice?" she called.
"Yes?"

"Do you know where this came from?" Mrs. McMillan brought the envelope out to Ms. Appleby's desk.

After the assistant shook her head no, the headmistress carried the envelope back to her own office, opened it, and discovered the microcassette. Curious, she placed it in her recorder, then closed the door to her office before pushing the play button. Mrs. McMillan listened to the tape three times before buzzing Ms. Appleby on the intercom.

Cleo and Robbi arrived at school, outwardly calm but dying to know if their plan had worked. Everything hinged on the cassette tape being audible and believable.

"You know in a way that little audio tape was probably better," said Robbi. "I mean, Mrs. McMillan doesn't have a VCR in her office, but you said she's got a microcassette player. There's no reason she won't be able to listen to it before she counts the votes."

Cleo nodded her head as she opened her locker. "I hope so," she said, laughing nervously. "If she buys it, we can thank my father's lousy memory for the idea."

A moment after the first class began, an announcement came over the public address system. It was the headmistress.

"Good morning, students. This is Mrs. McMillan. I want to tell you that although I had expected to have the results of the student body election by second period, there are unforeseen circumstances which will delay the tally of the vote. I promise, however, the results will be made public by noon today. Thank you."

The murmuring started immediately, everyone coming

up with their own ideas about what had happened. Though Cleo tried to mask her jitters, she dropped her pencil four times until Dr. Smith asked her if anything was wrong. It couldn't have been much worse if Cleo had been running for office herself.

Class was agonizingly slow, but then Mrs. McMillan made a second announcement asking Charles Maxwell, Andy Monahan, and Michael Payton to report to her office immediately.

Robbi leaned across the aisle to Cleo and whispered, "Busted!" She was beaming and Cleo couldn't help smiling back.

The level of chatter went up by decibels. Everyone sat up and strained to look out the door, hoping to catch a glimpse of the boys as they made the long march to the office.

Cleo wasn't quite sure how she survived the next few hours. Though she managed to end up in all the right classes, she barely heard a word any of her teachers said. *What happened in Mrs. McMillan's office this morning?* she wondered. The suspense was driving her mad.

Finally, in the middle of fourth period, Mrs. McMillan came "on the air" again. One by one, she announced the results of the election. She went through the winners for representative, treasurer, secretary, and vice president. Before the last category she paused for effect, "And for president of our student body, the winner is . . . Jason Garrett."

Cleo practically jumped out of her seat. They had actually done it. For the rest of the class she sat up much straighter and even managed to concentrate on a few things her teacher was lecturing about.

At lunch Cleo hurried to find Robbi. "We did it," they exclaimed, dancing around each other and jumping up and down. But their victory ritual wasn't complete without Jason, and they tore off to find him.

Their comrade was holding court before his many supporters in the lunchroom, but the second he saw the two girls, he excused himself from his fans and headed toward them.

"Well, I guess everything worked out, thanks to you," he said, smiling at Cleo. "And you, too, Robbi. Shall we have lunch together?" The three kids found an empty table but it soon was mobbed by Jason's fan club. Cleo felt herself shrinking down in her seat, feeling obviously out of place. She ate her lunch quietly, too uncomfortable to take part in the conversations. As she looked around, she noticed that Charles and his friends were nowhere to be seen. *They must be hiding*, she thought.

"Can we meet after school?" Jason asked the two girls at the end of the lunch period. "I'm afraid we really didn't have much of a chance to chat just now."

Cleo and Robbi looked at each other, then back to Jason and nodded their agreement.

About half an hour into the next class, there was another announcement from Mrs. McMillan. This time it was to call Cleo Oliver to the office.

Cleo was sure she was going to faint. Just when she thought she had gotten away with the whole charade, she had been found out. She tried to think of excuses for being in school last night, for cutting classes yesterday morning, and more, but her brain was completely fried. The sound of someone's throat being cleared snapped Cleo out of her daze to find Robbi was tapping her lightly on the shoulder with a pencil, and the entire class was staring at her.

"Cleo? Did you hear the announcement?" her social studies teacher asked, giving the girl a very worried look. "You should go to Mrs. McMillan's office right away."

Cleo blinked, then stood and headed to the door. This time she made a conscious effort to stand tall. She knew she had done nothing wrong, not really, so she decided she would hold her head up proudly as she went to her fate.

"Hello, Cleo," said Ms. Appleby when Cleo came in the office. "Go right on in. She's expecting you."

The assistant didn't sound or look ominous. *Maybe it's not so bad,* thought Cleo and as she opened the door she forced a smile. Mrs. McMillan was seated behind her desk, reading through some papers.

"Hello, Cleo. Please have a seat." The woman put the papers facedown on the desktop. "I don't know how you knew, Cleo, but you were right about certain students fixing the election. Based on an anonymous tip, I had Mr. Slovenski cut the lock from Charles Maxwell's locker. We discovered a bag of ballots—the originals that he'd stolen. Apparently he replaced them with others showing him to be the landslide winner." Mrs. McMillan shivered then looked up at Cleo. "I just want to apologize for not believing you."

Cleo broke into a tooth-baring grin. She wasn't in trouble after all. Undercover Cleo could keep her secrets.

"Thanks, Mrs. McMillan." Cleo squirmed in the

chair, hoping to be excused so she could go back to class.

But Mrs. McMillan twisted the gold chain on her glasses and leaned forward. "I wanted to ask you though, might you know anything about the events that took place in my office last night? Someone exposed these boys by leaving a tape recorder running. 'Old Lady McMillan,' indeed," sniffed the headmistress, who had clearly been insulted by the title Charles had given her.

"Anyway, obviously someone else besides these hooligans spent some time in my office last night. Do you happen to know who that might have been, Cleo?" asked the administrator, who was studying every nuance of the girl's face like a hawk watches a juicy mouse.

By now, however, Cleo was a pro at playing poker face. "I can't help you there, Mrs. McMillan," the girl said, "but I'm sure glad someone was around to catch the bad guys." She smiled sweetly. "Did you have pizza for lunch? It smells great." Cleo opened her eyes wide in expectation of the woman's response.

The headmistress suspected the girl knew a lot more than she was letting on, but she couldn't very well force Cleo Oliver into confessing a noble deed. Besides, she had to admit, the girl did look completely innocent as she sat there playing with her silver locket. All of a sudden Cleo's gesture triggered something in Mrs. McMillan's memory.

"How strange, I saw a necklace very similar to yours not that long ago. Now where on earth was that?" the woman wondered.

Cleo swallowed hard as she looked down at the locket. "You mean this? Oh, practically everybody's got one,

Mrs. McMillan,'' she lied. "You can find them all over the Village." Greenwich Village was a mecca for the latest in teenage fashions.

Mrs. McMillan nodded her head. "Maybe that was it," she said, sounding unconvinced. She was trying to dredge up her vague memory of the locket when Ms. Appleby buzzed.

"Mr. Slovenski's here to see you, ma'am."

"Thank you, Alice. I'll be just a moment," said the headmistress. She turned back to Cleo. "That'll be all for now, and, Cleo . . ."

"Yes, Mrs. McMillan?"

"Thank you again. This has certainly proved to be a lesson for me, which is very rare these days."

Cleo popped out of the chair and headed for the door, almost running into the custodian on his way in. "Hi, Mr. Slovenski," she said, and on impulse, she gave him a quick peck on his leathery cheek.

The man stood in shock for a second before he growled, but by that time Cleo was skipping down the hall. Mr. Slovenski stared after her, wondering what was going on. It was the second time in less than twenty-four hours that a young girl had behaved strangely around him. First, there was that featherbrained Julie and now a student he didn't even know. It had to be the weather.

Mr. Slovenski did his best to compose himself before his meeting with the headmistress, but no matter how hard he tried, he just couldn't stop a smile from spreading over his goggle-eyed face.

Chapter 29

Right after last period, Cleo and Robbi met Jason as he came down the wide staircase. He was still being congratulated by everybody and the number of kids coming up to pat him on the back made Cleo wonder if anyone at all had voted for Charles.

A moment later Jason joined the girls and gave them both a warm broad smile that was better than a thousand spoken thank yous.

"Where *is* Charles Maxwell?" asked Robbi. She laughed. "Boy, did he mess up big-time. Couldn't even win by cheating."

"He's got to be wondering what happened to his plan," said Jason. "And by the by, what was Charles talking about last night? The bit about Mr. Fleming's test being in my pack?"

The girls looked at each other before Cleo answered,

"You know, I don't have a clue about that."

"Yeah, me neither," piped in Robbi, "but thank goodness, whatever they were up to, it didn't work."

The three friends continued making their way toward the front gates when they noticed Mr. Slovenski carrying a bucket full of large sponges. He was making a weird cackling noise as he hurried upstairs.

"Am I wrong," asked Robbi, "or did that classify as laughter and a smile?"

Cleo stared after the man. "Kinda scary, huh? I wonder where he's going?"

"Come on," said Robbi. "He's just too happy, we've got to check this out," and she rushed after the custodian, not even bothering to see if her friends were behind her.

They followed the man up to the sixth floor, being careful to hang back far enough so that he wouldn't notice them. The custodian went straight into the gym and the threesome hurried from the stairwell to peek in the door.

Charles Maxwell, Andy Monahan, and Michael Payton were toeing a line in front of Mr. Slovenski. As they listened to the man's instructions, their heads were hanging, and they all seemed to have shrunk by a good six inches.

"My dad'll never understand this," murmured Charles. He looked like he was about to cry as he and his friends rolled up their sleeves and each took a sponge out of the pail that Mr. Slovenski now placed in front of them.

"I can't tell you how pleased I am that you boys have 'volunteered' to help out around Walton," said the custodian. "I've got an exciting and very educational list of projects lined up for you." The man cracked his knuckles and stuck his face up close to Charles. "I have a feeling this is going to be the year that you boys really learn something valuable in school."

Mr. Slovenski finally had the crew of floor waxers he wanted. As the three boys got down to begin scrubbing, the man hit them with one more tidbit of information. "Do you kids really think I wasn't on to you? I knew you'd been in my workshop, because I saw the coffee you spilled in there last week. I just didn't figure on you being so brazen as to climb in through my window. Your job tomorrow is going to be taking that window out and scrubbing off all the rust with a toothbrush."

The man threw back his head and laughed. "Nobody can fool Old Slovenski, no siree, bob."

Robbi giggled into the palm of her hand and Cleo dragged her two friends away. "I think we've seen enough."

"Yeah," said Jason. "What do you say we drop by Ye Olde Pizza Palace for a spot of refreshment." His suggestion was met with eager approval and before long the three friends were sliding into an empty booth at their favorite hangout.

"Here's to success," said Robbi, lifting her water glass. " 'Crime doesn't pay' they always say and we-'ve proved they're right." The trio clinked their glasses in a toast.

It was definitely a time to celebrate and they all ordered ice cream sundaes. Cleo couldn't help feeling a little sad at the thought that she wouldn't need any more disguises. It had really been fun the past two weeks, but now her precious makeup box from Jean-Luc would only be used for pleasure, not "business."

Partway through her sundae, Robbi put down her spoon. "Um, I've got to get home. I just remembered, I'm way behind on my math homework." The girl extracted a few dollar bills from her jeans pocket and slapped them on the table. "This should cover mine," she said, wriggling out of her seat.

Cleo opened her mouth to say something, but Robbi stopped her with a pointed look. Cleo knew that her friend had to be up to something because Robbi always, always finished her math homework during study period. This could only be some sort of lame excuse.

"Rob," Cleo suggested, "just a few minutes more and I'll be done, too. We'll leave together."

"No. No time. I've got to go," and the twinkle in Robbi's eyes told Cleo that begging was useless. The small girl scampered out of the restaurant, weaving her way through the harried servers.

Cleo and Jason sat alone at the table and for the next few minutes she concentrated intently on her sundae. Then after a while she stole a glance at Jason. He was looking straight at her and smiling.

"By the way, Cleo . . . are you busy Friday night?" he asked.

Cleo, in an attempt to finish up quickly, had just stuffed a huge spoonful of ice cream in her mouth. All she could manage to do was shake her head no.

"Well, I was wondering if you, and Robbi, of course, would like to come to my party? I know I didn't invite you before, but I really didn't know you then, and if it's not too late, I'd like you both to come.'' He sped through his words and spoke in such a soft voice that Cleo had to lean in to hear him. Then he paused and calmed himself with a sip of water. ''Actually, I was rather hoping you would be my . . . well, my . . . my, uh, date.''

Cleo could scarcely believe her ears. She nodded her head and didn't even try to stop the huge smile that was spreading from one side of her face to the other.

''Super,'' Jason beamed, and immediately spilled chocolate sauce all down the front of his shirt.

Cleo stifled a chuckle and after looking at the stain he had just left, Jason let out a loud laugh, too. ''Guess I was a bit more nervous about asking you to my party than I thought,'' he said.

Cleo was totally flattered. It was hard for her to believe anyone could ever be nervous at the idea of talking to her. The ice broken, she and Jason had a great time talking and finishing every bite of their sundaes.

After paying their bill, the kids stepped outside The Pizza Palace where Jason turned to Cleo. ''Shall I walk you home?'' he asked.

Cleo giggled. It sounded so old-fashioned, but she had to admit, it also sounded pretty nice. ''Sure,'' she said, glad to have the afternoon go on a little longer.

When Jason finally left her standing in the lobby of her apartment building, Cleo was already thinking about the new problems in her life—one that was tough but not altogether unpleasant.

Now she would have to figure out how to play the most difficult role of her life—Cleopatra Elyse Oliver.